About Shoma Narayanan

Shoma started reading Mills & Boon® romances at the age of eleven, borrowing them from neighbours and hiding them inside textbooks so that her parents didn't find out. At that time the thought of writing one herself never entered her head—she was convinced she wanted to be a teacher when she grew up. When she was a little older she decided to become an engineer instead, and took a degree in electronics and telecommunications. Then she thought a career in management was probably a better bet, and went off to do an MBA. That was a decision she never regretted, because she met the man of her dreams in the first year of business school—fifteen years later they're married with two adorable kids, whom they're raising with the same careful attention to detail that they gave their second-year project on organisational behaviour.

A couple of years ago Shoma took up writing as a hobby—after successively trying her hand at baking, sewing, knitting, crochet and patchwork—and was amazed at how much she enjoyed it. Now she works grimly at her banking job through the week, and tries to balance writing with household chores during weekends. Her family has been unfailingly supportive of her latest hobby, and are also secretly very, very relieved that they don't have to eat, wear or display the results!

TM

Secrets & Saris

Shoma Narayanan

MILLS & BOON

First published in Great Britain 2013
by Mills & Boon, an imprint of Harlequin (UK) Limited.
Harlequin (UK) Limited, Eton House, 18-24 Paradise Road,
Richmond, Surrey TW9 1SR

© Shoma Narayanan 2013

ISBN: 978 0 263 23495 4

Harlequin (UK) policy is to use papers that are natural, renewable and recyclable products and made from wood grown in sustainable forests. The logging and manufacturing process conform to the legal environmental regulations of the country of origin.

Printed and bound in Great Britain
by CPI Antony Rowe, Chippenham, Wiltshire

Also by Shoma Narayanan

Take One Arranged Marriage…
Monsoon Wedding Fever

Did you know these are also available as eBooks?
Visit www.millsandboon.co.uk

TM

To Vishpala and Paramita for being my sounding boards
for every book I write and to Malini for being
my sounding board for pretty much everything else!

CHAPTER ONE

'IN THE EVENT of a water evacuation…'

The stewardess's voice droned on and Shefali leaned back in her seat and shut her eyes. Water evacuation, indeed! Unless they crash-landed in a river it was very unlikely they would need life jackets during this flight between one completely land-locked city and another. She winced. If there was only some way to block out all *sound*. Her head was pounding like crazy, and she had to stop herself from opening her bag and digging out yet another painkiller.

'Cabin crew to stations for take-off,' the Captain's voice said over the plane's PA system, and Shefali's eyes flew open.

She looked out of the window involuntarily. It wasn't the first time she'd seen Delhi from a plane window— there had been trips to Mumbai, to Thailand, even to Paris—but this time she was leaving for good, and she couldn't help but feel a lump in her throat.

The comfortable-looking matronly woman in the seat next to Shefali gave her a reassuring smile. 'Flying for the first time?' she asked.

Shefali shook her head. She didn't want to spend the two-hour flight making polite conversation, and this lady looked the chatty kind. Before Shefali could shut her eyes again, she had started.

'Are you from Delhi or Jabalpur?'

'Neither,' Shefali replied.

But the lady wasn't about to give up. 'Going for a wedding?' she asked, pointing at the henna tattoos that covered Shefali's hands.

Shefali pulled the long sleeves of her shirt down a little further to hide the elaborate designs that extended all the way up her forearms. The traditional *mehandi* ceremony had been held three days before her wedding-that-never-happened, and she'd had to wait for hours afterwards for the henna paste to dry. The rich black had now faded to orange, but to Shefali's paranoid eyes her hands and arms still screamed out *jilted bride*.

'Excuse me a second,' she muttered, and pressed the button to call the flight attendant. 'Can I shift to a seat in the emergency exit row?' she asked when the attendant came up to her. 'I have a…a knee problem. I need more leg-room.'

She picked up her handbag and moved gratefully to the seat pointed out to her. It was an aisle seat two rows ahead, and the window seat next to it was occupied by a man around her age who was peering intently into his laptop screen.

Shefali was fastening her seatbelt when the man spoke without looking up from the screen.

'So where *are* you from, then? If you're not from Delhi or from Jabalpur.'

She gave him a startled look. 'I'm sorry?'

The man turned, and Shefali saw his face for the first time. He was quite strikingly good-looking, with blue-grey eyes and perfectly chiselled features. For a few moments Shefali found herself staring stupidly without a word to say. Fortunately he gave her a quick smile and turned back to his computer.

'I couldn't help overhearing,' he said, and lowering his voice. 'Good thinking with the knee problem.'

'Thanks,' Shefali said. 'I think.'

The man nodded and started typing something into the computer. He didn't seem disposed to talk any more, and Shefali felt a pang of something approaching disappointment. A random conversation with an attractive stranger might have helped take her mind off things. But who was she kidding? Nothing could take her mind off the single, mind-numbingly humiliating fact that her fiancé hadn't bothered to turn up for their wedding. The wedding that she had spent the last year planning and preparing for.

Sometimes it felt as if her whole life had been geared towards that one day when she'd marry the perfect man and settle down into happy domesticity. And Pranav *had* seemed perfect when her parents had introduced him to her. He was rich, successful, and very attractive—and though it was to have been an arranged marriage she'd very quickly started weaving him into her daydreams. Finding out on their wedding day that he'd decided to go back to his ex-girlfriend had been the biggest shock she'd ever had in her sheltered and slightly pampered life.

The attendant brought across their pre-ordered lunch trays. Her neighbour closed his laptop and took his. Shefali shook her head abruptly.

'No, thanks,' she said. Her head was still aching, and even the sight of food was off-putting.

'Can I have it?' the man next to her asked. He gave

her a quick grin. 'I missed breakfast—and, well...' He gestured towards his tray. 'This doesn't look like enough to keep a mouse alive.'

'OK,' Shefali said, taking her tray from the attendant and passing it on. His hands were good, she noticed. Strong, with square-tipped fingers, sinewy wrists and no rings. She'd never liked Pranav's hands—thin and hairy: an awful combination. Pity they hadn't been grounds enough for her to decide against marrying him.

'You're sure you don't want any of this?' the man was asking, gesturing towards the two trays.

Shefali barely repressed a shudder. 'I'm sure, thanks. Just the bottle of water, please.'

He handed it to her, and she took it, carefully avoiding touching his hand. His proximity was affecting her weirdly, and she didn't want him to notice. Her head still ached, and she picked up her bag, rummaging around in it for the package of painkillers. They seemed to have vanished, so she pulled out her table and starting putting the contents of her designer bag on it one by one. The painkillers finally turned up, wedged between the pages of the novel she'd been too stressed to take out and read. Heaving a sigh of relief, she popped open the blister pack and put one into her mouth.

She hadn't opened the bottle of water yet. She tried to twist it open, but the seal stubbornly refused to break. And the pill she'd put in the centre of her tongue—because, according to her primary school science teacher, there were no tastebuds there—was slowly dissolving in her saliva and spreading to parts of her mouth where there *were* tastebuds. It tasted vile.

'Ugh,' she said, as politely as she could to the man next to her.

He had stopped eating and was staring with horrified fascination at the heap of things that had emerged from her bag.

'Ugh,' she said again, and finally nudged him with her elbow and pointed at the bottle.

'Oh—sorry,' he said, taking the bottle from her and opening it with an effortless twist of his wrist. 'Here you go.'

She grabbed it from him with more haste than grace and took a few rapid gulps. The pill finally went down, though it cleaved lovingly to the roof her mouth for as long as it could. She made a face—the bitter taste in her mouth was refusing to go away.

'Have some sugar,' the man suggested, giving her a little sachet from one of his two lunch trays.

His voice was perfectly grave, but he was laughing, his eyes crinkling up at the corners in the most attractive way possible. His teeth were perfect, Shefali noticed. Having gone through years of painful and extremely expensive orthodontic treatment to achieve her own current flawless smile, she resented people who'd been born to have perfectly aligned teeth. He looked as if he'd never had to go to a dentist in his life.

Her neighbour polished off his second dessert and handed the empty trays to one of the stewards. 'We've almost arrived,' he remarked, looking at his watch, and the seatbelt sign came on as if on cue.

Shefali didn't answer, but clenched her hands unconsciously. This was it, then. The start of her brand-new life. In a few minutes they'd be landing in a city where no one knew about her engagement and the disastrous end to it, and she could make a completely new start. She'd never taken her job very seriously—teaching at a playschool had been just something she did to fill the time between graduation and marriage—but when she'd wanted to get out of Delhi it had been her boss who'd come to her rescue, offering her the job of centre manager at their Jabalpur branch, and she was determined not to let him down.

Neil Mitra was looking at his neighbour curiously. There was something odd about her—some kind of pent-up anxiety that came through in her strained expression and rather jerky movements. Also, from what he'd been able to see of the packaging, the pills she'd been popping were either anti-depressants or pretty strong painkillers. If not for the haunted look in her eyes she'd be an attractive girl—she had neat, very regular features, a flawless complexion, and rather nice eyes with lovely long eyelashes.

'Everything OK?' he asked quietly as the plane came to a halt and girl tried to jerk to her feet without undoing her seatbelt.

'Yes, of course,' she said, but her voice sounded artificially cheerful.

Her glossy, perfectly styled hair fell across her face and hid her expression as she bent to open the recalcitrant catch of her seatbelt. Finally getting it undone, she stood up and opened one of the overhead lockers, tugging valiantly at her bag. After watching her struggle for a few seconds, Neil got up to free it for her. She was taller than he'd thought, just half a head below his own imposing six-foot two inches. The flowery scent from her hair teased at his nostrils, and for a second their eyes met and held as he took the case out and handed it to her.

Shefali looked away first, flustered by her reaction

to him. Perhaps she was going crazy, she thought, suddenly furious with herself. Pranav's betrayal was making her overly susceptible to the slightest bit of attention from any good-looking man. She tried to take a step away from him, but there was nowhere either of them could move—everyone in the plane was standing in the aisle, trying to get at their luggage, and the doors hadn't opened yet.

'Relax, I don't bite,' he said, sounding amused as he noticed her trying to move away.

Shefali flushed angrily. It was bad enough realising how pathetic she was without him noticing too. Luckily the doors opened just then, and she was able turn towards the exit.

'Here—let me take that,' he said, leaning down to take the handle of her case from her.

Relinquishing it, she followed him into the airport, her nose wrinkling just a little as she noticed how tiny it was.

Neil grinned at her reaction, Neil grinned. 'Doesn't match up to Delhi T3, does it?' he asked.

Refusing to be embarrassed any further, Shefali shrugged. 'It's quaint,' she said. 'Oh, look—my cases are here.'

Neil helped her get the bags off the carousel, his smoky blue eyes widening as he realised how many there were. 'Arctic expedition?' he asked, his brows quirking up.

'I'm moving here for work,' Shefali said stiffly. 'Two of the cartons are full of educational aids I'll need for my job.'

It had taken her days to pack, choosing between sentimental reminders of her growing-up years in Delhi and more practical things like dishes and clothes. And then her boss had landed her with the two cartons to carry, airily offering to pay for the extra baggage. The last thing she needed now was to be given grief for the amount of luggage she had. She eyed his mid-sized rucksack contemptuously—he was probably carrying clothes for a two-day trip, and she had her entire *life* in her bags.

Suddenly overcome by the enormity of what she was doing, she shoved her remaining bags onto the trolley and said gruffly, 'Well, thanks for everything. I guess you need to head off now…'

Looking slightly taken aback, Neil gestured towards the trolley groaning under the weight of three cases, two large cartons and a carryall. 'Are you sure you'll be able to manage that?'

'Perfectly sure,' Shefali said, dredging up a polite little smile, though her heart sank into her shoes at the thought of having to wrestle with all that stuff on her own. Then her sense of pride reasserted itself. She wasn't *helpless.* She'd be fine. She didn't need help from random strangers, however good-looking they were. 'Thanks again for your help,' she said, trying to sound as gracious as possible. 'I'm sure we'll see each other around, this is such a small place.'

'It has a population of over a million,' he said drily. 'But if we do run into each other I'll come across and say hello.'

Someone from the throng of people outside the airport yelled, 'Neil—over here!', and the man gave Shefali a brief nod before turning away.

Flushing, Shefali watched him stride off, his broad, athletic frame a stark contrast to the frankly pudgy man with a ponytail who'd greeted him exuberantly as soon as he'd stepped out.

He was nowhere in sight when Shefali finally managed to get her trolley out, but by then she had other things to worry about. The airport seemed to be in the middle of nowhere. Apart from a small car park there was nothing—trees and more trees surrounded the area, and there was not a cab in sight. Everyone else who'd got off the flight was being met by someone, and the couple of auto-rickshaw drivers who were hanging around looked as if they spent their spare time mugging little old ladies and stealing candy from kids.

She looked around a little helplessly—the man Neil was driving out of the airport in a black SUV, and she wished she'd asked him for a lift.

'Need a lift somewhere?'

Shefali turned to look into the concerned eyes of the motherly woman she'd been sitting next to at first. Shefali shook her head. The woman seemed nice enough, but she reminded her way too strongly of all the curious aunties back in Delhi, who'd been simultaneously horrified, pitying and excited at her wedding being called off.

In her hurry to get away Shefali beckoned to the least ruffianly-looking of the auto-rickshaw drivers and gave him the address of her hotel. The auto was cramped—her bags took up most of the back seat of the three-wheeler—and she had to sit to one side, almost falling out of the open vehicle as it zipped through almost deserted roads. For a while she tried to look out and interest herself in her surroundings, but then her shoulders slumped and she leaned back in the seat and closed her eyes. The first day of her new and independent life had been exhausting, to say the least.

CHAPTER TWO

'THIS IS…REALLY impressive,' Shefali said, barely able to conceal the surprise in her voice.

Mrs Dubey, the outgoing centre manager of the play-school, smiled. 'Not as villagey as you expected, then,' she said, her voice dry.

Shefali turned around quickly. 'Oh, no—I didn't mean that!' she exclaimed, though it was exactly what she'd meant and they both knew it. 'It's just that the centre looks so much like the one I worked in when I was in Delhi—at least from inside. And there's so much space outside. You actually have a full-sized playground for the children. It's lovely!'

There was enough genuine enthusiasm in her voice to win Mrs Dubey over, and her smile became a lot warmer. 'I'm glad you like it,' she said. 'On Monday I'll introduce you to the staff and take you through the paperwork, then you'll be all set. I don't think there's anything else we need to cover now. What are your plans for the rest of the day?'

Shefali looked a little lost. It was a Saturday, and Mrs Dubey was right—without either the teachers or the children around, there wasn't much for her to do here. 'I'm not sure,' she said. 'I'd assumed this would take a lot longer. Can I start moving my things into the flat today?'

The playschool was a two-storey building, and the upper storey had a decent-sized flat that came with the job. It had looked rather nice when Mrs Dubey had shown her around earlier, and Shefali was looking forward to moving in.

Mrs Dubey was shaking her head, though. 'I still need to move some of my boxes out,' she said. 'I'm staying with friends for the next few days, before I head out to Pune to join my son, so I'm getting the bigger things packed today and sent on directly. And we did say that you'd move in tomorrow.' Her face brightened up. 'I'll tell you what you can do,' she said. 'My car's free—the driver can take you for a drive up to the river. The Marble Rocks and the waterfall are lovely, and you won't get a chance to do any sightseeing once you get caught up with schoolwork.'

It sounded as good a plan as any—and it would definitely beat spending the rest of the day in her hotel room brooding. The couple of quick internet searches that she'd done before she'd left Delhi had touted the stretch of the River Narmada running past the city as one of the most beautiful and unspoilt river views in the country.

An hour later, however, she was frowning as she stood at the riverbank. What she could see of the river as it meandered between tall cliffs of white marble was stunning. But the point of coming all this way had been to take a boat ride through the cliffs, and that was one thing she was apparently not going to be able to do. Every single boat seemed to have been commandeered by a TV crew that had set up operations on the riverbank.

'But why can't you rent me *your* boat?' she asked one of the boatmen.

He shook his head firmly. 'They've paid all of us to keep off the river while shooting is going on,' he said self-importantly.

'I need to speak to someone in charge,' Shefali said, and before the man could stop her she had pushed through the crowd gawking at the cameras.

No one objected—probably with her 'big city' looks they thought she was part of the crew. At any rate, she managed to grab the sleeve of a harried-looking girl who was standing by the side of one of the cameras holding a large sheaf of papers.

'Are you part of the crew?' she asked, and the girl nodded. 'I understand that you've paid the boatmen so that they won't take any boats out. Is that correct?'

'That's right,' the girl said, sounding wary now.

'Look, I'm here on a very short trip, and I was really keen on a boat ride,' Shefali said rapidly. 'Is there any way I could take one of the boats out for a short while? Maybe when you're taking a break or something?'

'I'll have to ask Neil,' she replied. '*He* told us not to let any of the boats go out.'

At the name Shefali automatically looked at the crew, scanning through the faces. There he was, just a few feet away, she realised. Her tummy did an involuntary flip-flop of excitement. The man from the flight, looking even better now, his hair ruffled by the breeze and his tanned biceps exposed in a short-sleeved white T-shirt.

'Who's he?' she asked the girl in an undertone.

The girl looked surprised. 'Neil Mitra,' she said. 'He's the anchor for our show.'

What show? Shefali felt like asking. They were from a TV channel, that was obvious—there was enough branding around to convert the entire city to single channel viewership—but... 'I don't remember seeing him in anything,' she said instead. 'Is he well-known?' Neil's looks were too unconventional to fit in the film-star category, but she could imagine him being a hit on TV, with his direct eyes and quirky smile.

'No,' said a voice near her ear. 'Not at all. Now, if you'll excuse us, we really need to begin shooting. We lost two days while I was in Delhi.' He nodded at the girl, who backed away, looking flustered.

'I'll get the guys together, then,' she said, and made a rapid exit.

Neil turned to Shefali. Wild horses couldn't have dragged it from him, but he'd thought about her quite a bit since he'd last seen her.

'A very short trip?' he asked, his voice sardonic. 'I thought you'd moved here? Something to do with education if I'm not wrong?'

Damn—he'd overheard her earlier. Determined to brazen it out, Shefali lifted her chin. 'I meant it's a short trip to this place. It's miles out of the city, and I'm not planning to come here again in a hurry.'

Neil shrugged. 'Well, tough luck. I guess you'll have to get here some other day if you're really set on boating.'

'Or you could let one of the boatmen take me across when you're on a teabreak,' she suggested, keeping her voice even. He seemed to be being difficult for no reason at all.

'Or you could watch a film of the cliffs,' he said.

Shefali glared at him, and Neil gave her an unapologetic grin. 'It's not about when you leave,' he said. 'It's about when you come back. You could land up bang in the middle of a take and ruin it for us.' He thought for a bit. 'Look, the waterfall is on a different section of the river—maybe if you go there and come back in a few hours we'll be done.'

'All right,' Shefali said, and turned to go. She had no intention of coming back—not while Neil was around at any rate.

Neil watched her leave with mixed feelings. There was something about the girl that got to him. Probably the air of privilege that surrounded her—she assumed that people around her would do what she wanted. And she'd been pretty dismissive at the airport when he'd only been trying to help her. In stark contrast to the way she behaved, though, was the look in her eyes, which was guarded and vulnerable at the same time.

'You can take a boat out if you want,' he said finally, just before she went out of earshot. 'Only don't wave wildly at the cameras or anything.'

Strongly tempted to tell him that she had no intention of looking at his precious cameras, Shefali nodded politely and waited while he beckoned one of the boatmen over and gave him a few quick instructions in Hindi. If he was expecting her to fall at his feet in gratitude, he had a long wait coming.

Once they were a few hundred metres from the bank, she turned to look at Neil. He was with the TV crew, busily arranging the next shot, and he seemed to have forgotten all about her. Frowning, Shefali turned back and tried to concentrate on the boatman who was giving her a long and, she suspected, almost completely fictional history of the region. The cliffs were impressive, though—not the pure white she'd expected, but pale grey and massive, looming over both sides of the river.

The boatman was still talking half an hour later, when the boat came back to the small wooden jetty they'd started from. Shefali stood up gingerly, almost losing her balance as the boat rocked under her.

'Need a hand?' an amused voice said, and she looked up to see Neil standing by the riverside.

They seemed to be done with the shoot—the camera had been packed up, and Neil looked far more relaxed than he had earlier.

Not wanting to fall over on her backside and make a fool of herself, she took Neil's outstretched hand and allowed him to pull her out. Electricity zinged between them and Shefali felt her skin heat up. He seemed quite unaware of the effect he had on her, releasing her hand as soon as she was on dry ground.

'Come on, I'll introduce you to the crew,' he said, and then smiled slightly. 'It'd help if I knew your name first, though.'

'Shefali,' she said. 'Shefali Khanna.'

'Well, hello, Shefali Khanna,' he said gravely. 'Meet Rafiq, our director.' He waved at the pudgy ponytailed man who had come to pick him up at the airport. 'And this is Priti...' The girl she'd spoken to earlier bobbed her head at Shefali with a quick smile. 'And those scruffy guys over there are Animesh and Sohail.' The cameraman and his assistant, who were both almost as well turned out as Neil, gave him indignant looks.

'We're the actual stars of the show,' Animesh said.

'This guy just hangs around and shoots his mouth off in front of the camera.'

Neil laughed. 'Back in a minute,' he said. 'I need to pay the boatmen and figure out tomorrow's schedule.'

Sohail followed him, and Shefali was left with Rafiq and Priti. 'What's the show about?' she asked.

'It's called *Soul of the City*,' Rafiq said. 'We're doing twelve episodes in twelve different cities. Here—take a look at some of the stuff we've done for one of the earlier episodes,' he said, holding out an iPad to her. 'This was in Vizag.'

'It's very rough,' said Priti, the girl she'd spoken to earlier. 'The final edit still needs to be done. But it gives you the feel of the thing.'

It certainly did. It cut between interviews with college students, politicians and housewives, with bits of local music interspersed with breathtaking footage of beaches and hills. And Neil was amazing—he looked even better on camera than he did in real life, and he managed to connect with each and every person he interviewed.

'This is great stuff,' Shefali said once the clip was over. 'You guys are incredibly talented.'

Rafiq gave her a smug look. 'Of course we are,' he said. 'And having Neil striding around and looking like God's gift to womankind doesn't harm our ratings either.'

'Is this his first show?' Shefali asked curiously.

Priti looked surprised. 'You really don't know who he is, do you?' she said.

Shefali shook her head.

'He's pretty well known,' Priti said. 'Been with the channel for almost three years, and he's had two very successful shows recently. Of course they're on fairly serious themes, but he handled them brilliantly.'

She named the shows, but clearly she didn't expect to Shefali to recognise them. Shefali wasn't sure whether to be annoyed or amused by Priti's slightly patronising tone. She didn't watch TV at all, except for the movie channels, and she had no idea if the shows Priti was talking about were big league or not. For all she knew they aired at ungodly hours, and only housewives who were very, very bored or very, very frustrated watched them.

Neil was standing next to her again. 'Coffee, anyone?' he asked.

Priti shook her head vigorously. 'We need to wrap up some still shots of the river before the light goes. But we don't need you for that—you and Shefali go ahead.'

'Come on, then,' Neil said. 'Unless you're in a hurry to get back?'

Shefali shook her head again. She hadn't seen the waterfall yet, nor the temple with the sixty-four statues of dancing girls that Mrs Dubey had been raving about, but she'd have to come back some other day.

Probably it was the effect of the sun, but she was terribly conscious of the man next to her as she climbed the stairs leading to the main road. She surveyed him from under her lashes. He was quite amazingly good-looking, she decided, though his looks were unconventional. His hair was a rich brown, with a couple of gold streaks in it. It was an unusual colour—most Indian men had jet-black hair or, more rarely, sandy-brown. His skin was tanned a perfect golden brown, and he had a square jaw with a cleft chin, and uncompromising, steady blue-grey eyes.

Trying to distract herself, Shefali stopped a couple of times to look at the carved stone figurines being sold at the stalls lining the stairs. There was a little marble one of Ganesha, the elephant-headed god, which she picked up and looked at for a while before putting it back.

'Don't you want it?' Neil asked.

'My mum collects them,' Shefali said. 'But it's going to be a while before I see her again, so there's no point buying it now.'

'Won't she come and visit? Check on how you're settling in and stuff like that?'

'According to her, moving here is the dumbest thing I've ever done in my life,' Shefali said drily. 'She's planning to stay put in Delhi and wait for me to come to my senses.'

'Ahh—like that, is it? Do you miss her?'

Shefali shook her head. 'Not really. Oh, look at that!' 'That' was an intricate carving of an elephant, displayed in the window of the next stall. It was pretty enough, but really she'd pointed to it only to distract Neil from the conversation.

He gave it a considering look. 'Bit lopsided, if you ask me,' he said. 'And I've never seen an elephant with quite such beady eyes.'

Shefali laughed, and they climbed the last few steps to the road.

Neil looked around. 'You know what, I don't think there's a single decent café around here,' he said.

'I'm OK with tea at one of those *tapri* stalls around the corner,' Shefali said, but Neil shook his head. 'Now who's being a snob?' Shefali asked teasingly.

'That would be me,' Neil said. 'I'm a little fussy about the kind of tea I drink. Cold drink instead? Or, if you're done here, we can head back to the city and grab a coffee there?'

'Heading back to the city sounds like an idea,' she replied. 'Should I meet you there? I borrowed a friend's car, so I'll have to go back in that.'

Only the driver was nowhere to be found, though the car was still parked in the spot where Shefali had got out. After several attempts to locate the driver had proved fruitless Shefali left a note on the windscreen and gratefully accepted Neil's offer of a lift.

'I wonder where he could have got to?' she fretted as she got into his dangerous-looking SUV. 'He doesn't have a mobile, and he told me he'd stay in the car.'

Neil shrugged. 'Must have wandered off for a smoke. Message your friend and tell her you're OK—I assume he'll contact her when he does go back eventually.'

Shefali dutifully shot off a message to Mrs Dubey, and then leaned back in the passenger seat, yawning hugely. It had been a long day, and she was tired. The emotional strain of the last few weeks in Delhi was catching up with her, and she felt exhausted all the time.

'Close your eyes and take a nap,' Neil suggested, sounding amused. 'It's a long drive.'

It was dusk by the time they finally pulled up in the city centre, and Shefali's eyes blinked open as the car came to a stop. Realising that she'd taken Neil at his word and slept blissfully all the way back, she jerked upright, feeling embarrassed and hoping she hadn't snored or drooled all over the seats.

'It's past seven—coffee or an early dinner?'

'Both,' Shefali said. 'I need to wake up.'

Looking back, she knew that was the moment she should have said she was tired and wanted to go to her hotel. But the thought didn't cross her mind. The attentions of a man as attractive as Neil were flattering after what she'd been through, and besides, she couldn't bear the thought of having to go back to her dreary hotel room.

The little café they went to was full of young couples—most of them looked like college students who'd sneaked off for a date without their parents knowing. Neil got them a table near a window and then went to fetch their coffees.

Shefali watched him as he stood at the counter. He was far and away the best-looking man in the place, and something like pride stirred in her chest as she watched several women give him the once-over and then glance across at her to see who he was with.

'Here you go,' Neil said, reaching across the table to set her cappuccino in front of her.

He settled into the sofa opposite her and Shefali couldn't help but notice the breadth of his shoulders and the way his T-shirt strained across his muscles as he leaned back. She looked quickly at his hands. No rings. She definitely wasn't in the market for anything serious—not for a long, long while—but some harmless flirting wouldn't do her or her self-esteem any harm.

'So, tell me more about what you do,' Neil said. 'College professor? Coaching sweatshop?'

Shefali shook her head, laughing.

'All through college I wanted a teacher who looked like you—I never was lucky enough,' he said.

'I work with kids,' Shefali said. 'Who don't care how I look. But I'm not really a teacher any more—it's more administrative work.'

'Do you like kids?' Neil asked.

Shefali hesitated. All her life she'd made a point of saying the correct thing. It had been drilled into her so thoroughly that it had become a part of who she was. Maybe it was time to start saying what she actually thought for a change.

'I hate that question,' she said. 'No one asks *Do you like adults?* do they? I love working with children, and I like most kids just the way I like most adults. But kids are human beings too, and there are some who're perfectly obnoxious.'

Neil laughed. 'Well, that's honest, at any rate,' he said. 'And where are you working now?'

Shefali leaned forward. 'Let's not talk about work,' she said. 'It's unlikely we'll meet again—you'll be out of here when your shoot is done, and I'm going to live here for a while—let's talk about stuff we wouldn't discuss with anyone otherwise.'

Neil raised his eyebrows. 'Like...?' he asked. He was always wary of women who tried to get too close too quickly. So far one of the main attractions Shefali had for him was that she wasn't throwing herself at his head the way most women did.

Shefali picked up on his hesitation and said, 'Don't worry—I'm not talking about a Freudian psychoanalysis session. Just general stuff. Nothing personal. Like what I told you about not always liking kids.'

Neil relaxed a little. OK, not so dicey, then. She was just amusing herself. Just as well—he was beginning to find her quite disturbingly attractive, and the lighter they kept things the better.

'You first or me?' he asked.

'You first,' Shefali said. 'One deep dark secret that you've never told anyone else.'

'I'm petrified of dogs.'

Shefali laughed. 'Come on—you made that up! You're the outdoorsy kind. There's no way you'd be scared of a dog.'

Neil shook his head solemnly. 'When I was about two years old I was playing in a sandpit and this massive Alsatian came along and knocked me over and put its paws on my chest. I was lying there for some five minutes before someone noticed me and called the dog off.'

Shefali's eyes softened. 'That must have been awful!' she exclaimed. 'Poor you! No wonder you don't like dogs—that experience must have traumatised you for life.'

'Actually, it didn't,' he said, his grey eyes dancing with amusement. 'My mum was the one who was traumatised—I dusted myself off and went away to play on the slides.'

Shefali gave him a playful punch in the arm—involuntarily she noticed the strength of the muscles under the warm velvety skin. 'You wretch!' she scolded. 'For a minute there I actually felt sorry for you.'

Neil raised his hands. 'Sorry,' he said. 'It was too good to resist.'

'OK, a real one now.'

He leaned back, his long strong body stretched out against the sofa. 'Let me think. I like pink.'

'Very poetic,' she scoffed. 'Come on, Neil, be serious here!'

He grinned. 'I'm not good with parlour games.'

Bedroom games were probably more his thing. The thought popped into Shefali's mind out of nowhere and she gave herself a quick mental shake. That line of thinking wasn't going to get her far. Perhaps spending time with Neil wasn't such a good idea after all—he was a little too good-looking to be a soothing companion.

'OK, here's one thing,' he was saying.

Shefali stopped thinking to listen.

'And it's really something I've never told anyone before.'

She raised an eyebrow enquiringly.

'When I was fifteen I watched this movie about a diamond heist and it was pretty inspiring, I guess you'd say. So I thought I'd stage a mini-heist of my own. I crept out in the middle of the night and broke into a neighbour's house. Only I didn't have the guts to steal anything valuable so I raided their refrigerator instead.'

'I hope you had a good meal,' Shefali said gravely.

'I fed the food to the cat,' Neil admitted. 'That's one more thing—I grew up in Bengal but I hate fish. And that's all they had in their fridge.'

'*Aren't* you Bengali?' Shefali asked, surprised. 'Your surname sounds pretty typically Bengali.'

'Dad is,' Neil said. 'Mum's British.'

That explained the light eyes and chestnut hair, though his skin was as tanned as any Indian's.

'Did they meet in Kolkata?'

Neil shook his head. They'd met in Oxford, apparently, where Neil's father had been studying, and they'd had an extremely tumultuous courtship. When they'd finally got around to getting married they'd returned to India to look after the tea estates that belonged to Neil's father's family.

Neil told the story well—not surprisingly, given that he made his living talking into a camera. She hardly noticed the time go by, and it was dark when they finally stepped out of the coffee shop.

'The restaurant I know is not too far,' Neil said. 'Are you OK with walking, or do you want to take the car?'

'Walking's fine,' Shefali said. 'I'm a bit tired of sitting around anyway.'

She was acutely conscious of his nearness, of his arm brushing lightly against the sleeve of her *kurta*, and the smell of his woody cologne. The pavement wasn't too well-lit, and Shefali stumbled slightly at one point. Neil put a hand under her elbow to steady her and she shivered at the unexpected contact.

'You OK?' Neil asked.

She nodded, hoping he didn't realise how close she'd come to flinging herself into his arms.

'Just a little tired, I think,' she said.

'I guess you're not used to spending so much time in the sun?'

'I'm not,' she said ruefully. 'That's why I fell asleep in the car—I must look a real mess.'

'You look beautiful,' Neil said abruptly.

Shefali looked up in surprise at the unexpected compliment.

They were in a rather deserted lane, between two rows of closed shops, and in the orange glare of the streetlights her upturned face was pale and so breathtakingly lovely that Neil lost his head. He put a hand under her chin and turned her face up. Unhesitatingly, he bent down to press his lips to hers.

The kiss came as such a shock that Shefali stood absolutely still for a few seconds. The sensation was indescribable. She'd been kissed before, but the feel of Neil's warm, demanding lips on hers was something else altogether. Involuntarily she clutched at his arms, trying to pull him closer. His hands were cupping her face now, and with a little inarticulate cry Shefali arched her body to lean in closer to the kiss. She was conscious of nothing other than the feel of Neil's lips on her mouth and throat.

A lot of time seemed to have gone by when Neil let her go finally, and she stared at him, her eyes still a little hazy from the effect of his kisses. One of his hands came to rest lightly on her shoulder and the other caressed her cheek. He ran a thumb gently over her lower lip.

'I should apologise,' he said softly, and his voice was not quite steady. 'I shouldn't have done that. But I'm not sorry I did.'

She wasn't sorry either, she realised. The kiss had healed something in her—helped her to start thinking of herself as an attractive, desirable woman once again. Pranav's desertion had shaken her self-confidence badly, and she could only feel grateful to Neil for having given some of it back. But she'd only just met him, and the sudden attraction between them was something she was completely unprepared for. She needed to think.

'I have to go,' she said quietly.

Neil reached out quickly to take her hand, making her quiver with longing all over again.

'Are you upset about this?' he asked. 'We both got a little carried away, but it's not the end of the world.'

In spite of what he'd said, he was beginning to regret kissing her. He'd been very careful over the last four years not to get involved with anyone, and the momentary madness that had overtaken him was completely uncharacteristic.

'I'm not upset,' Shefali said, but her eyes were troubled. Three weeks ago she'd been ready to marry Pranav and spend the rest of her life with him. Now she was perfectly happy standing in a lane in a strange city kissing a man she'd just met—what did that make her?

'Come on—let's have dinner and I'll drop you back to your hotel afterwards,' Neil said.

Shefali followed him into the restaurant. It was a rather silent meal. Neil seemed to have withdrawn into himself, and Shefali began to wonder if he was, after all, having second thoughts. Maybe her reaction had been a little too abrupt. She would have explained if she could, but the whole thing with Pranav was still too recent to discuss over dinner with someone who—kiss or no kiss—was virtually a stranger. Especially when the well-fed family at the next table was doing its best to listen in to every word they said.

'Shall we?' Neil said smoothly, once he'd paid the bill, and Shefali trailed behind him to the car park rather like Mary's little lamb.

He didn't ask for her number when he dropped her off, and she didn't volunteer it or ask for his. Presumably if he wanted to speak to her he would call the hotel. She was moving the next day, but she'd leave a forwarding address.

The sun pouring through cheap lace curtains woke Shefali on Monday, and she sat up with a muffled groan. She'd had a bad night, disturbed by dreams in which Pranav and Neil had alternately abandoned her at the altar. The last dream had ended with Pranav being eaten by a crocodile, which was distinctly weird—her subconscious was obviously taking the whole thing very seriously.

Shefali rubbed her eyes. The lace curtains would need to go—it was only six-thirty, but the room was flooded with light. Thick *khadi* was what was needed— or maybe blackout blinds if homespun cotton wasn't available. And the walls were an awful colour—something between pistachio-green and olive. Mrs Dubey, though a wonderful person, had rather peculiar tastes in home décor.

Sighing, she got out of bed. It was the first day of actual school, and she needed to be on time. She'd spent Sunday moving her things from the hotel to the flat, and buying essentials like groceries and buckets and mops. In spite of the amount of work she'd done she'd kept thinking of Neil. That kiss had been pretty amazing. In retrospect it was probably the best kiss of her life, and she couldn't help fantasising a little.

The rest of the morning was so busy she didn't have time to think of anything other than learning the ropes at the school. Mrs Dubey was obviously a competent administrator, but her management style resembled that of an Army drill sergeant—most of the younger teachers looked relieved at the thought that she'd be leaving soon.

'I think you'll be settled by the end of the week,' Mrs Dubey said as she stood next to Shefali, watching the children filing out. Each child had been given a note to carry home that explained that Mrs Dubey was leaving and introduced Shefali as the new centre manager. 'I'm around for the next couple of days in any case, if you need anything.'

Shefali gave her a smile that she hoped looked grateful enough. She was exhausted and, truth be told, beginning to wonder if moving here had been such a good idea after all. Unlike the Delhi playschool she'd

worked at, this one was fully self-contained—she'd have
to manage the billing and all the financials in addition
to supervising the teaching, and it looked like a lot of
work. The kids were rather sweet, though, and a lot
less smart-alecky than the Delhi brats she was used to.

'Nina, stop—you need to take this letter and give it
to your mum,' Mrs Dubey said, holding back a bright-
eyed little moppet who was rushing past.

'Can I give the letter to my dad instead?' Nina piped
up. 'My mum isn't here, and he's always around.'

Mrs Dubey looked mildly scandalised, but Shefali
smiled at the child. 'Why not?' she said. 'Does he come
to pick you up?'

'Yes,' she said and pointed towards the school gate.
'Look—there he is!'

Shefali turned. There was only one man in the crowd
of parents thronging near the gate—tall, with rumpled
chestnut hair and familiar mocking eyes. Maybe Nina's father was standing further back—but what was
Neil doing here? She'd not told him where she worked,
though he could have probably found out from the hotel.

She gave him a wary look as he walked up to them,
but his attention wasn't on her.

'Hi, pumpkin,' he said, ruffling Nina's hair and in-
clining his head ironically at Shefali.

'Daddy!' Nina squealed happily, and clung on to his
hand.

Neil Mitra—married with a kid. Something he'd ne-
glected to mention even after he'd kissed her. No wonder he'd been in such a hurry to get away. It still seemed
incomprehensible, though. For one thing he looked so
young—she'd assumed that he was around the same
age as she was. But he couldn't be. Nina was one of

the bigger kids at the playschool, and had to be at least four years old.

'*You're* her father?' Shefali asked finally, looking him up and down.

'So I've been told,' Neil drawled. 'I've been thinking of getting a DNA test done, but you know how things keep getting put off.'

Shefali was about to snap at him when she realised that Nina was right next to them, listening intently.

'He *is* my dad,' Nina said, her voice firm, but Shefali saw her chin wobble slightly. 'What's a DNA test, Daddy?'

'A piece of paper that says you're all mine,' Neil replied, his voice rough as he swung Nina up into his arms. For a few seconds he'd been so intent on getting under Shefali's skin that he'd forgotten his daughter was within earshot. 'But we already know that, so we don't need one. Bad joke. Sorry.'

'Well, now that I see you together I can tell you're father and daughter,' Shefali said, trying to lighten things up a little. She'd have a lot to say to him if she saw him alone, but now was most definitely not the time. 'Your ears are identical.'

Nina chuckled happily. 'Everybody says my *eyes* are like Papa's,' she said.

'Don't believe, them. Yours are much prettier. Your ears, on the other hand…'

'I can't believe it—a schoolmarm with an ear fetish,' Neil murmured as Nina slipped down from his arms.

'I read it in a Sherlock Holmes story,' Shefali said, blushing hotly. 'Ears are supposed to show a family resemblance the most.'

'*The Adventure of the Cardboard Box*,' he said, and

he smiled suddenly, his eyes lighting up in the way that made Shefali's heartbeat quicken. 'It's years since I read Conan Doyle.'

'Same here,' Shefali, said, and there was a little pause broken by Nina's cheerful little voice.

'Teacher, I *love* the patterns on your hands,' she said. 'They're like a *dulhan's* hands. Did you just get married?'

The henna again. Shefali wished there was a way of getting it off—nail polish remover? Acid, maybe? Anything to get rid of the orange designs snaking over her hands, a constant reminder of her stupidity.

For the moment, though, she was done with lies and evasions. Neil could think what he liked.

'I almost did,' she said. 'But it didn't work out.'

Neil's brow furrowed. 'Get into the car, sweetheart,' he said to Nina. 'Look—Bela Mashi's waiting for you by the gate.'

Nina gave Shefali a cheery wave and ran off. Neil's amazing eyes were troubled as he turned back to Shefali.

'Look, I'm sorry,' he said awkwardly. 'I didn't realise...'

Shefali cut him off. 'It's OK,' she said quickly. 'I didn't realise you were married for that matter. Maybe you'd forgotten it for a while as well? Look, I need to go—I've got some people to meet.'

She turned and almost ran up the steps. It was perfectly true—she *did* have a meeting with the man who did the accounts for the school. Only she didn't go straight to the office. Instead she headed quickly for the back stairs and went up to her flat. Once inside, she held her hands up to her flaming cheeks. God, how *stupid* she was. It hadn't even occurred to her that Neil could be married. He definitely hadn't acted married. But then Pranav hadn't acted madly-in-love-with-another-woman either. Maybe it was something wrong with *her* that made her the automatic choice for every man with a secret? And she'd spent the entire weekend thinking about Neil—she'd even daydreamed about him in class today, for heaven's sake. It all went to show that she didn't have the first clue about men, and the less she tangled with them the better.

Downstairs, Neil stood in the playground for a bit, hoping Shefali would reappear so that he could explain himself. When it became apparent that she wouldn't, he turned and walked back to his car. Inside, Nina was bouncing up and down excitedly, telling her nanny about her day. Neil's grim expression softened as he looked at the two of them. Bela Mashi had been his nanny when he was young, and she'd come out of retirement when Nina was born. He didn't know what he'd have done without her—especially after Reema had left.

'Daddy, isn't the new teacher *pretty*?' Nina asked.

Neil smiled at her reflection in the rearview mirror. 'Very,' he agreed. 'Is she teaching your class?'

Bela Mashi shook her head before Nina could say anything. 'Centre manager is what she is. Going to run the school after that Dubey lady retires. Young girl like that—what does she know about running a school? Anyway, we're leaving in a couple of months. Doesn't matter to us. It's the others who'll be stuck with her. And she's from Delhi too. God knows why she's come to work in *this* little village.'

'Little village' was how Bela Mashi described all the cities Neil had chosen for his latest show, but she followed him loyally wherever he went. Starting the car, Neil wondered what he'd have done without her. Probably buckled under family pressure and let his sister bring up Nina. Not that he hadn't been tempted by the offer—bringing up a baby alone wasn't the way he'd imagined spending the best years of his life. But that was the point, he mused, glancing at Nina as she tugged open her bag to show Bela Mashi something she'd made in class. The last four years with Nina *had* turned out to be best years of his life, though not quite in the way he'd dreamed of in his teens.

CHAPTER THREE

IT WAS ALL the fault of the stepladder she'd found tucked away in the storeroom, Shefali decided. The second she'd seen it she'd been reminded of all those paint ads in which glamorous models and actors transformed a room with a few strokes of a brush. Reality wasn't quite so much fun. For one, the ads never showed the hours you needed to put in, first scraping the old paint off and then smoothing the walls with messy Plaster of Paris. Or that ceilings were unreachable even after she'd tied the brush onto the end of a broomstick.

She'd been at it for almost the entire day now, trying to transform her pistachio-green walls to a more cheerful pale yellow. So far she'd done exactly one third of one wall of the living room, having given up on the ceiling. In any case the ceiling was white—it didn't matter if it looked slightly dingy. The colour on the walls would brighten everything up.

She was just dipping the brush into the paint when the door bell rang. Who could it be? She put the brush on its side and covered the paint tin exactly as they'd shown in the video on house painting she was using as her reference material. Then she pulled off the old *dupatta* she'd tied around her head and went to open the door.

Neil Mitra.

She felt the breath catch in her throat at the sight of him leaning against the door. The sun was setting somewhere in the distance and his brown hair glittered golden. While his face was in shadow, his eyes sparkled as he broke into a disarming smile.

Realising that she was still staring at him like a dork, Shefali cleared her throat. 'Yes?' she said, putting on her best dealing-with-irritating-parents expression—neutral, but completely in charge of the situation. It probably didn't go very well with her paint-splattered T-shirt and jeans, but she could hardly run in to change.

'Is this a bad time?' Neil asked, his grin broadening as he peeked around her into the living room.

The furniture was swathed in the lace curtains that she was planning to get rid of anyway, and the step-ladder stood perfectly aligned with the wall. OK, the room wasn't exactly ready to be featured in a home décor magazine, but she couldn't see what there was to grin about either.

'It's fine,' Shefali said, not budging from the door-way. 'If you're not going to take too long?'

'I won't,' Neil promised. He'd thought about this for a whole week before he'd decided to come and speak to her. 'I just wanted to let you know—I'm not married.'

Right. Thrown off-balance more than a little, Shefali stared at him uncertainly. 'You mean…Nina isn't your daughter?'

'She is.' Neil gestured behind her. 'Do you think I could come in? It's a little weird, having to blurt out the story of my life on your doorstep. I'm a very shy guy, really.'

'Really?' Shefali said, but she stood aside to let him in. Her head in a bit of a whirl, she gestured towards the dining room. 'We can sit here.'

Neil strode across the room, and Shefali took a minute to admire his athletic body from the rear.

'I'm divorced,' Neil said, as soon as he sat down, his blue-grey eyes looking up into hers.

Oh. For some reason that hadn't occurred to her. She sat down opposite him, unconsciously smoothing her long T-shirt over her knees. 'How long ago?'

'Very soon after Nina was born.'

'And Nina's been with you ever since?' Fathers very rarely got custody of the kids in a divorce battle, Shefali knew, and getting custody of a baby girl only a few months old had to be even more uncommon.

Neil shrugged. 'Reema didn't want her. We got married young, had a child early. She wasn't ready for that kind of commitment.'

Shefali stayed silent, not sure how to react. She was hugely relieved, of course, to learn that she hadn't kissed a married man. For the entire week she'd been seeing herself as a home-wrecker who encouraged philandering husbands. But the fact that he wasn't married also meant that he was available, and she didn't want to think of him that way. This part of her plan to get over Pranav didn't involve men. And especially not madly attractive men like Neil.

The madly attractive man in her dining room was now surveying his surroundings. 'A bit grim, isn't it?' he asked, gesturing around at the bilious walls and the mildewed framed posters of kittens in baskets.

'That's why I'm repainting it,' Shefali said drily. 'To make it a little less grim.'

'Have you ever done anything like this before?'

She shook her head. 'I've lived in my parents' house till now. They're not really the do-it-yourself type.'

'I wouldn't have put *you* down as the do-it-yourself type either,' Neil remarked.

Shefali bristled immediately. 'I'm not incapable!' she said.

'Not at all,' he said smoothly, but Shefali got the impression that he was still laughing at her. 'It's just that every time I've seen you so far you've struck me as someone who doesn't push her boundaries too much.'

Kissing a man she barely knew had definitely pushed her boundaries, and Shefali found herself resenting his remark.

'Was that all, then?' she asked. 'You came to tell me you're not married? I don't mean to be rude, but I really do need to get on with my painting.'

'I'll help you,' he said easily. 'You've done most of the hard work anyway—it won't take long to get the room done. And there are a couple of other things I want to talk to you about.'

Shefali gave him a cold nod.

'Well, the first thing is that Nina's taken quite a fancy to you.' Neil said. 'And she's a little upset because she says you've been ignoring her. Apparently on the first day you spent quite a bit of time talking to her, but since then you've not spoken to her at all.'

Shefali felt her face heat up. She'd deliberately avoided Nina, feeling awkward about the whole thing with Neil. It had been unfair of her, but she hadn't realised that Nina had noticed.

'Look, I can understand why,' Neil said. 'The whole episode that night—I lost my head a little, and I'm sorry. Really, really sorry. I can now understand why you probably don't want to see me again, with your wedding having just been called off... But I don't want Nina to be affected by something that's totally my fault.'

He was making her sound like a neurotic on the rebound. Plastering an over-bright smile on her face, she said, 'Of course not. Nina's a lovely kid. I'm sorry if she thought I was ignoring her—it's been a crazy week. I'm still settling in, and of course I was feeling a little awkward about...you know...'

Her voice trailed off, and he nodded understandingly. 'I had no idea you were going to be working in the school, otherwise...'

This time, it was his turn to leave a sentence hanging, but Shefali knew what he meant. If he'd known she was going to turn up in his daughter's school he wouldn't have come within a mile of her.

'So that's settled, then,' he was saying. 'I promise to behave myself from now on, and you'll treat Nina like any other student. I'm not asking for special attention—she can be a real brat sometimes.'

Remembering how she'd told him that she disliked some children, Shefali said quickly, 'Oh, she's a wonderful kid—very bright and enthusiastic, no trouble at all.'

'Not obnoxious?' he asked, his eyes laughing at her. 'Like some adults?'

'Not at all like some adults,' she said, getting to her feet. 'Listen, if you're really planning to help with my room we need to get going.' She wasn't sure if she wanted him around, given the effect he had on her hormones, but help with her painting was help with her painting. Difficult to get and impossible to refuse.

'I'll help,' he said. 'But one last thing—will you be OK with doing a small appearance on my show?'

Whatever she'd expected him to ask, it wasn't that.

'Appear on your show doing what?' she asked.

'Well, you're a bit of an oddity, you know,' he said, walking into the living room and picking up the can of paint and a brush. 'A girl from Delhi, coming to live in a small town—you could say what you think of the place, tell people what made you decide to come here and so on.'

'I chose this town because nobody knows me here,' Shefali said abruptly. 'And because I wanted to get away from everyone I know in Delhi. That's not going to sound good on national television, is it?'

'Hmm,' Neil said as he got on the stepladder and started to paint the top part of the wall with wide brush-strokes.

He was *good*, Shefali thought, admiring the way the muscles in his back rippled as he moved the brush back and forth.

'What about a short piece on you doing a make-over on your flat? We can get some of the crew to help you, and it'd look good.'

'I don't think so,' Shefali said. 'I really don't want people back home to know what's happening in my life.'

'Right,' Neil said. 'I guess that's understandable. Can you pass me the roller, please?'

Shefali handed it to him, and then asked, 'How come you've put Nina in school here if you're only going to be around for a couple of months?'

'That's the good thing about your playschool—you

have branches everywhere,' he returned. 'I've been transferring her from one branch to another for the last year. But I'm done with this kind of life now. In two months we'll be back in Mumbai, and she'll join regular school. I'll shift to an assignment that doesn't need me to travel.'

That made sense, Shefali thought as she picked up a brush and started work on the lower part of the wall. It was just that the responsible dad side of him was so incongruous with his rather Bohemian appearance.

'How old are you, Neil?' she asked, and he stopped painting to look down at her.

'Twenty-eight,' he said. 'Why?'

'It's just that you seem too young to be the father of a four-year-old,' she said. 'I thought maybe you were older than you looked. But you're not—you're just a year older than I am. Most men your age are still out having fun, and you're looking after a child…'

Neil shrugged. 'Life doesn't turn out according to one's plans, does it?' he said.

Unsure whether he might be making a dig at her own circumstances, Shefali continued painting in silence.

After a bit, he asked, 'Tell me again—why aren't you getting the painting done by someone else?'

'Too expensive,' Shefali retorted. At the disbelieving look he gave her, she said, 'The school doesn't pay me a fortune, you know.'

Neil frowned. 'I would have sworn you were pretty well-off.'

'My parents are. But I'm not really on talking terms with them any more. They weren't OK with the idea of my leaving Delhi to come and live here. So I need to live within my means.'

He was still frowning. 'Are you seriously saying you're planning to spend the rest of your life here, managing the school?'

'I haven't started thinking about the rest of my life yet,' Shefali said. 'I'm still trying to come to terms with the fact that I'm not going to be Mrs Shefali Mehrotra. I was brought up to be a pampered trophy wife, and I don't really know what I'm going to be now that Pranav Mehrotra's out of the picture.'

'Pranav is the guy you were going to marry?' Neil asked, and then, almost in the same breath, 'Pass me the smaller brush for the corners, please.'

Shefali nodded and passed him the brush. Clearly the story of her life wasn't engrossing enough to capture Neil's full attention.

He carefully finished doing the corner between the ceiling and the wall he'd just finished painting, and then got down from the stepladder.

'Arranged marriage?' he asked, picking up the ladder to move it in front of the next wall.

'Yes,' Shefali said. 'Only in the end Pranav figured he'd rather be cut off from his parents and marry his ex-girlfriend than marry me and be heir to his family's millions.'

'Pretty courageous decision to take,' Neil said thoughtfully.

Shefali looked at him, so indignant that she was at a complete loss for words. Whose side was he on?

Neil went on, 'Why did that make you leave home, though? The break-up wasn't your fault, and you couldn't have been in love with the guy.'

Put like that, her decision to move did seem rather drastic. 'He chose the day of the wedding to let me know,' Shefali said tightly. 'Everything was ready—I'd even changed into my wedding *lehnga* when his father called mine to say that Pranav had left Delhi with his ex. It was…' She took a deep breath. 'It was the most humiliating experience of my entire life. Most of the guests had arrived already, and we had to tell them all the wedding was off. My parents had spent a fortune on the arrangements, and that went to waste as well. It was worse afterwards—there were people sniggering and pointing fingers wherever I went. I couldn't take it any more.'

'What about your parents?' Neil asked. 'Weren't they supportive?'

'My parents were soon pushing me to marry another guy,' she said. 'One of Pranav's friends—he proposed pretty soon after Pranav didn't turn up for the wedding. It was ridiculous. One of my aunts actually suggested that we go ahead with the wedding, only with this other man as the groom.'

Neil winced. He could see now why she'd left, and while she might not appreciate being told so right now he thought she'd had a lucky escape.

'So you wanted to get away from it all?' he asked.

'Sort of,' Shefali muttered. 'I was already working for the playschool in Delhi—the owner of the chain is a friend—and my Dad thought it a "suitable" job till I got married. So I asked my boss if I could have my old job back, and then it occurred to me that it might make more sense to move out of Delhi for a while. My parents went mental when they heard. They said it was like an admission of defeat, that I should get married as soon as I could and there were already people spreading rumours that the break-up was my fault. So I told them to stuff it and left.'

Neil smiled briefly. 'Good decision.' He hesitated a little. 'Listen, if you need help on anything at all, don't hesitate to ask me. I'm sorry I made fun of you about doing the painting yourself—I didn't realise you were short of cash.'

Not wanting him to labour under a false impression, Shefali shook her head. 'I'm not poor or anything—my grandma left me a heap of money when she died, and I've got that tucked away safely. It's just that when all this happened I realised that I had to prove to myself at least that I could manage on my own. Even without my grandmother's money. And, let's face it, she would have left that to my brother rather than to me if she hadn't had a massive quarrel with him.'

Embarrassed at having said so much, Shefali picked up her paintbrush and started slathering paint on the wall.

Neil went back up the stepladder, but after while he said softly, 'You're pretty amazing—you know that?'

Startled, Shefali almost dropped her brush as she turned to look at him.

He gave her a quick smile. 'I mean it. I'm not the kind of person who hands out empty compliments.'

That she could believe—if anything, he erred on the side of brutal frankness.

'Thanks,' she said, and Neil grinned at her.

'Let's get the last wall done with and then I'm off,' he said. 'I need to pick Nina up from a friend's house.'

CHAPTER FOUR

'So HE SAID that when my hair grew out I should tie the front part of it back and the layers would become more defined,' Shefali said, peering into the mirror worriedly. 'That doesn't seem to be happening.'

Neil tried valiantly to control his expression, failed, and burst out into laughter.

'Get it cut,' he said. 'I'm sure the city has at least one decent hairdresser.'

'But I always…' Shefali said, and then, seeing the ridiculous side of what she'd been about to say, started laughing. 'You're right,' she said. 'It's just hair—if they mess it up it'll grow back again.'

'Right,' Neil said. He reached out a hand and solemnly prodded her cheek.

'What are you *doing*?' Shefali asked, jerking back and swatting his hand away.

'Checking if you're real,' he said, his eyes glittering. 'You're so perfect I was expecting plastic.'

She glared at him. It was a week since he'd helped her out with painting her living room, and he'd come over twice after that, with Priti and a couple of other guys from his TV crew who'd drunk large quantities of *nimbu paani* and helped her get the rest of the flat painted. Today she was going with him to attend a class reunion at a nearby school—one of the ex-students in town for the reunion was a Bollywood actor who had made quite a name for himself playing character parts, and Neil was interviewing him for his show.

'You're the one who told me to dress up a little,' she said indignantly.

'But you're perfect all the time,' Neil protested. 'Perfect swingy hair, perfect make-up, perfectly ironed, perfectly *fashionable* clothes, perfect shoes— *Ow*, perfect aim with a hairbrush...'

'You deserved that,' Shefali told him sternly as she took her hairbrush back, but she was smiling.

The more she got to know Neil, the more she liked him. He continued to be brutally frank about everything, but he was helpful, funny and incredibly loyal to his friends. He also seemed to be incredibly unaffected by Shefali—it was as though that first kiss had never happened. The trouble was Shefali continued to find him as attractive as she had when they'd first met, and it was a little annoying and more than a little frustrating that he treated her like one of the guys. She still didn't think that she was ready for a relationship, but it would have felt good to think that he was holding himself back too, battling his feelings because the time wasn't right for either of them...

She bit the thought back with a sigh as Neil got off the sofa and said briskly, 'Come on—hurry up or we'll be late.'

The party was more fun than she'd expected. Most of the guests were in their early thirties, and they were a happy mix of people. And of course there was the actor—a dark-skinned man with an intelligent mobile face. He specialised in honest uneducated villager roles, and it came as a bit of shock to hear him speak perfect English. Neil and his crew were circulating among the guests, with Neil doing short interviews with each of them. Later he would cut and edit the segment to around three minutes, but he'd shot for well over an hour before he wrapped up and came to sit next to Shefali.

'Very bored?' he asked, *sotto voce*.

Shefali shook her head. 'Not at all. I spent a lot of time talking to a woman who's a major in the Army—very interesting the stuff she had to say. Her husband's in the Army too. And I met a chap who runs a consumer durables dealership. He said he'd give me a good bargain on a washing machine.'

Neil raised his eyebrows. 'You're buying a washing machine now? What happened to the austerity drive?'

'The washerwoman's ruining my clothes,' she said. 'Last week she put a red kitchen towel into the wash with my under-things, and I now have seven pink bras.'

'Dipping into the money your grandmother left you?' Neil asked, trying not to think about Shefali in a pink bra.

'No, I sold my engagement ring,' she said flatly. 'Before I left Delhi. He could hardly ask for it back.'

Neil's eyebrows arched up, and he said after a pause, 'Good for you. I hope you got a good price for it.'

'I got a damn good price for it,' Shefali said, her voice grim. 'I took a cousin of mine along to a jewellery store and we told the owner that his fiancée wanted an exact copy of my ring. He gave us an outrageous quote—then I asked him to buy the ring from me at that price.' A brief smile crossed her face. 'He haggled, of course, but I got a good deal more than I would have if I'd just gone and asked him to buy it.'

Neil didn't say anything, and Shefali gave him a hard look.

'Shocked?' she asked.

He shook his head, and then said, 'Well, just a little.'

Shefali shrugged. 'I may have been brought up to be merely ornamental, but I come from a family of diplomats. I can strike a good deal when I need to.'

Neil nodded. Shefali's family was pretty well-known on the Delhi political circuit. He'd begun to understand a lot better why she'd needed to get away. Her ex-fiancé belonged to a family of wealthy industrialists, and their break-up had caused a major stir in their social circle. Her background also explained her sometimes uptight attitude—she was accustomed to being 'on display' most of the time, and found it difficult to loosen up. It couldn't be more different from the way *he* had been brought up. Though his family was probably wealthier than hers, theirs was old money, and it came coupled with a fine disdain for other people's opinion of their private affairs.

'You know, you're lucky Pranav changed his mind when he did,' Neil said after a pause. 'I know you don't see it that way right now, but things would have been much worse if the two of you had actually got married.'

Shefali looked at him in surprise—this was a completely new point of view. 'It would have been better if he hadn't agreed to an arranged marriage when he already had a girlfriend,' she pointed out. 'Actually, it would have been even better if he hadn't had a girlfriend in the first place.'

Neil smiled slightly. 'Yes, well, what I meant was

that, given he did have one, it's good you didn't end up married to him.'

'Maybe,' Shefali conceded grudgingly. 'That's not the way my family saw it, though.'

'I'm surprised your father didn't want you to take up a career,' he said inconsequentially. 'You'd have done pretty well.'

Shefali shrugged. 'He has very strong views about a woman's place in the family,' she said. 'But if I'd insisted I don't think he'd have stopped me. The problem is that I just went along with whatever he planned for me.'

It was only part of the truth. She'd always dreamed of a perfect little family—husband, kids, the works. Her prospective husband's face had been hazy in her mind. She'd just assumed that her parents would find her someone suitable. The kids, on the other hand, had seemed very real: two boys and a girl, the centre of her existence. She hadn't even seriously considered a full-time career—it wouldn't have been fair to the hypothetical kids. Now she cringed at the thought of admitting to anyone that her life's ambitions had revolved around marriage and motherhood. She still wanted children—once she'd got her life back on track and found someone she could trust enough to marry.

She caught the bemused look on Neil's face and said impatiently, 'Not everyone's as clear about what they want as you are, Neil.'

He laughed, his white teeth gleaming. 'My family would split their sides laughing if they heard you say that,' he said. 'According to them, I'm the most directionless person to walk the earth.'

Genuinely surprised, she said, 'But why would they think that?'

'Probably because they've spent the last seven years watching me make a complete mess of my life,' he said drily. 'Quite unlike my sister, who's an unqualified success…'

'What does she do?'

'She's pretty much taken over from my father,' he said. 'She and her husband run our tea estates in Darjeeling. Her husband's Sri-Lankan, and he grew up on a tea estate too, so they're perfect for the job. I found it a little too staid and repetitive for my taste.' He paused and stared moodily into his glass. 'And then, of course, there was my extremely short-lived marriage.'

Shefali waited for a while, and when he didn't say anything she put a hand on his. He looked up, surprised, and she squeezed his hand gently and said, 'You can tell me. If you want to. God knows I've been pouring my woes into your ears ever since we met.'

Neil smiled and squeezed her hand back. Shefali felt a little thrill run through her arm, and she had to struggle to hide her acute awareness of the man across the table.

'It's not a very long story. Reema and I had been dating since our schooldays—our families were close, and everyone expected us to get married eventually. I'd just finished college, and I was thinking of going to the US to do an advanced course in film-making. Reema's parents wanted her to go abroad too, to study further, but she wanted to be a singer. She had a lovely voice, and she was training in Hindustani classical as well as jazz.'

'I thought you couldn't learn both together?' Shefali said, frowning. 'They're very different styles of music.'

'Reema was always the queen of having her cake and eating it too.' Neil's voice was light, but there was undertone of anger. 'Except when it came to being a wife and mother. Because when we found out that she was pregnant all she wanted to do was get rid of the baby and get on with her life.'

Shefali was scandalised, and she knew it showed on her face. She didn't know a single person who'd got pregnant out of wedlock.

'That was Nina?' she asked, hoping she didn't sound either fake or judgmental.

'That was Nina,' he agreed. 'I wasn't going to have any baby of mine done away with. We'd been careless, and the way I saw it we had to live with the consequences. My mother was the only one who backed me up, but I got Reema to marry me and have the baby. After Nina was born I couldn't force her to stay—and, honestly, by then I didn't want to be with her either. So when Nina was six months old we called it a day, and Reema left for New York to complete her studies.'

'And you had to bring up Nina alone?'

'My sister offered to adopt her,' Neil said. 'She's some years older than me, and her son is the same age as Nina—she said she could take care of both of them. I didn't want that though.'

Shefali frowned. She could understand his scruples about Reema undergoing an abortion—however she couldn't understand why a twenty-four-year-old single man would want to bring up a baby by himself when he had another option. 'Why?' she asked. 'Wouldn't that have been the best solution for both Nina *and* you?'

It was obvious that it wasn't the first time he'd been

asked the question, but she got the feeling that he'd never really answered it before.

'It didn't seem right,' he said hesitatingly. 'Reema had already left her. My sister would have looked after her well, but Nina would have grown up with the idea that neither of her parents wanted her.' He flushed. 'I couldn't do that to her. I might have been young and inexperienced and unemployed, but I was still her dad.'

Incredibly touched by the admission, Shefali reached out and squeezed his hand. 'You've had it tough,' she said.

Neil shook his head. 'Not really. I could have married again, of course, but after the whole thing with Reema I didn't want to risk it. It wouldn't be fair to Nina if I got messed up over a woman again. We're better off on our own.'

Shefali was about to reply when all conversation was rendered impossible by the DJ turning up the music and loudly exhorting everyone to get onto the dance floor. Neil raised an eyebrow at Shefali, but she shook her head. She'd had enough of the party, and dancing with a bunch of uncoordinated strangers wasn't really her thing.

Neil took her hand and led her out of the hotel where the reception was being held. The atmosphere had changed with his confession, and Shefali was acutely conscious of the hard length of his body as he walked next to her. And he wasn't treating her like a buddy either—the look he'd given her when they'd left the party showed that he was as conscious of the attraction sizzling between them as she was.

'What next?' he asked as they got into his car. 'We've

missed dinner—do you want to stop somewhere on the way home?'

'No,' she said. 'I had heaps of samosas and chicken tikkas. I won't be able to eat a bite.'

Neil grinned across at her. 'Then I guess you won't have space for ice cream either, will you?'

'There's always space for ice cream,' she said, trying to sound as dignified as she could and failing miserably.

He laughed outright and they drove to the nearest ice cream parlour. It was crowded with college students, and Neil stepped out and got them two cones. 'Don't drip ice cream all over the seats,' he warned. 'This is a hire car. I need to give it back in good condition when I leave the city.'

They ate their ice cream in companionable silence. His explanation of why he'd elected to bring Nina up by himself had left Shefali with a new feeling towards him—a mingled tenderness and respect that made for a dangerous combination with the strong attraction she already felt.

'You have an ice cream moustache,' Neil said, and when Shefali tried to rub at her mouth with a tissue he took both her hands in his and held them together while he leaned forward and very, very gently licked the ice cream off.

Too stunned to react, Shefali sat stock-still as he started the car and drove towards her flat.

'Why did you do that?' she asked shakily a few minutes later.

Neil shrugged. 'It seemed like a good idea,' he said. 'Look—we're almost at your place.'

'There's a cow right in front of the school gate!' Shefali squeaked in alarm, all thoughts of kisses driven out of her head by the sight. Cows were common in the city, and so were water buffaloes, and they roamed around the roads at will. Shefali still hadn't got used to them, though, and pointedly crossed the road whenever she saw a herd approaching.

'I noticed,' Neil said gravely. 'Maybe you could get out and shoo it away so I can park?'

'No fear,' she said promptly. 'You can get out and shoo it away yourself.'

'I believe they run away if you twist their tails,' he said, but he got out, and urged the cow away from the gate—without touching its tail—and opened the gate.

'You can go in now,' he called out. 'I'll leave from here. It's pretty late.'

Shefali hopped out of the car and came to his side. 'Won't you come in for coffee?' she asked shyly.

Neil shook his head. 'It's too late,' he said. 'And Nina's alone with Bela Mashi.'

Now he was definitely prevaricating. Emboldened by his stunt in the car earlier, Shefali leaned a little closer and gently ran a finger up his arm. 'Nina'll be asleep already,' she said softly. 'Come on. It's just coffee.'

With a strangled sound of submission Neil slammed the gate shut and followed her up the stairs to her flat. Once inside, Shefali turned to him and slowly put her arms around his neck. Neil started to say something, but she stood on tiptoe and effectively shut him up by pressing her lips to his. For a few seconds he stayed motionless. Wondering where she was getting the courage from, she parted her lips slightly and teased the seam of his mouth with her tongue. His reaction was instantaneous, and he plundered her mouth so eagerly that Shefali was soon gasping for breath.

Sanity returned for a few seconds when Neil drew his head back and said, 'Shefali, I'm not sure…' But she silenced him in exactly the same way that had been so successful the first time.

This time it was several minutes before Neil came up for air. And when he did he reached behind her and quickly latched the door. Turning towards her, he collected her up efficiently in his arms and strode through a succession of pale yellow rooms to reach her bedroom.

Later she thought that she couldn't have called a halt to it even if she'd wanted to—Neil had been like an unstoppable force of nature by then, and she'd trembled a little at the sheer strength of the passion she'd managed to unleash.

Whatever hesitation she felt was soon swept away by a tide of pure sensation—if there was some way she could bottle the feeling, she'd make a fortune—and then Neil started to strip away her clothes and his, and she stopped thinking altogether.

CHAPTER FIVE

IT WAS STILL dark when Shefali's eyes flew open, and she automatically reached out for Neil. But his side of the bed was empty. She sat up groggily, switching on her bedside lamp. Neil came in a moment later from the bathroom. He was wearing the jeans he'd worn the night before, and carrying his shirt over one arm. Bare-chested, with his hair still rumpled, he looked gorgeous, but his expression was way too serious.

'Good, you're awake,' he said, coming to her side and leaning down to give her a hard kiss. 'I need to leave now—I'll see you tomorrow.'

'Why d'you need to leave?' Shefali protested, her voice still thick with sleep. 'Can't you go in the morning?'

'I need to be at home when Nina wakes up,' he said. 'And if my car is parked outside your house in the morning we'll have created a fine scandal.'

Not having thought of that, Shefali floundered a little. 'We could say it broke down and you left it here and walked home?' she suggested.

'You won't be asked to answer questions about it in a court of law,' he said, and his voice was stiff, almost harsh. 'There'll just be a lot of unnecessary gossip, which you won't be able to contradict, and neither of us can afford that.'

Shefali looked up at him silently. She hadn't been thinking clearly. She hadn't been thinking at all. She'd never slept with a man before, and at some point, incredibly moved by the experience, she'd told Neil so. Judging by the way he was behaving now, it had most definitely been a mistake. Probably he was expecting her to become clingy and possessive, and he was trying to stave it off by making it clear that he didn't mean to hang around.

'OK, then, if you need to go, you need to go,' she said finally, amazed at how steady her voice was. Perhaps she'd missed her calling after all—she could have won an award for being so perfectly calm and collected when her mind was in such utter turmoil.

'See you, then,' he said, and there was a note of relief in his voice.

A minute later Shefali heard the front door close gently behind him.

Getting up to latch the door, Shefali caught a glimpse of Neil driving off. He looked older than his years and very grim. A far cry from his usual cheerful self.

It was four o'clock. Too early to start the day. But in her current frame of mind there was no way she could go back to sleep. Sitting down on the bed, she tried to sort out her thoughts. From a purely physical point of view the night had been amazing, and her body still ached pleasurably in unfamiliar places. If she could ask it if it wanted to repeat the experience, she was sure that she'd get a resounding yes—every cell in her body would be shamelessly willing to sign a petition to get Neil back into her bed.

Moving on to the more complex subject of how she felt about Neil, Shefali faltered. Her hand came up to brush tears away from her eyes impatiently. It was all very well trying to be calm and mature about the whole thing, but the impulse to throw herself on the bed and start howling was immense. Neil's evident eagerness to be gone had hurt her badly. He hadn't even thrown a casual endearment her way, and though he'd said he'd see her later she would bet anything he'd call her with a dozen reasons as to why they shouldn't be with each other.

Maybe he was right. They'd both been carried away by passion, but there wasn't really much point in a relationship that was geared to fail. Neil had a lot of baggage, and he'd already told her that he didn't want to marry again. For that matter, she wasn't sure if *she* wanted to marry either, or even become involved in a serious relationship. Theoretically, a light-hearted fling with no strings attached would have been the perfect recipe to get over Pranav. But if she extended that logic she'd need to have another fling to get over Neil—and something told her that getting over Neil would be a lot more difficult than getting over Pranav.

She could write Neil off as a therapeutic one-night stand, of course, only she wasn't ready to give up what they had together just yet. In spite of the risk it posed to her heart, a short fling seemed to be the only solution. She gave a little groan of despair. Life suddenly seemed terribly complicated.

Neil used his key to enter the house he'd rented for his three-month stay in the city. Once inside, he threw himself onto the sofa and buried his head in his hands.

What a mess. Sleeping with Shefali had been the farthest thing from his mind when he'd left home the evening before. He'd been attracted to her since the day they'd met, but he'd decided early on to keep things light between them. Well, he'd failed.

Shefali had crept under his defences without his even realising it. Or, no, that was an unfair thing to think—whatever had happened was completely his fault, and he needed to sort it out. And quickly, before Shefali ended up getting hurt.

The realisation that he was the first man she'd ever slept with had made him feel angry, humbled and terribly guilty all at the same time. Angry because if she'd told him earlier he wouldn't have let things go quite so far. Guilty because he now felt responsible for her, and he knew he couldn't give her the kind of relationship she deserved. And humbled because she'd trusted him enough, felt safe with him...

A door creaked open, and Neil looked up to see Bela Mashi looking out at him blearily.

'*Ki khoka?* You're still awake? Did you go to bed at all?'

Neil shook his head.

'I was working,' he said. Bela Mashi was used to the weird hours his job entailed—she wouldn't ask nosy questions.

'Get some sleep now,' she instructed, turning to go back inside. 'I'll take Nina to school in an auto—you can sleep late.'

It was good advice, but he didn't take it, going into the kitchen to make himself some coffee instead. He had a tough day ahead of him. They were doing some scenes around the history of the city and were going to be filming at an old fort that had belonged to a warrior queen in the sixteenth century. The idea was to recreate a small part of her battle to defend the kingdom, and they had a couple of professional actors and a whole bunch of locals playing the queen and her soldiers. It would be a long and tiring day, and in his current troubled frame of mind he wasn't looking forward to it.

'I won't be able to pick you up from school today,' he told Nina as her dropped her off at the school gate.

Shefali, thankfully, was nowhere in sight, and Nina's class teacher was at the gate, ushering the children in. Nina nodded and scampered in. Her teacher gave Neil a curious look—rumours of the amount of time the new centre manager was spending with him had already begun to circulate.

The shoot was gruelling—there was no other word for it. Neil could even bring himself to feel sorry for the actress who was playing Queen Durgavati as take after take was ruined by the over-enthusiastic local extras, who stopped whatever they were supposed to be doing to wave into the camera eagerly whenever it came near them. Shooting on a budget had its disadvantages.

Taking his phone back from Priti between shots, Neil scrolled through the calls he'd missed. There were none from Shefali—maybe she was waiting for him to call her. He looked up to see Priti regarding him steadily.

'Do you want to take a break?' she asked. 'Rafiq has this bunch under control now, and we don't need you for the next hour or so while we do the siege scene.'

Rafiq was more than capable of handling the scene. Nodding at Priti, Neil got to his feet. 'I'll see you guys in an hour, then,' he said.

The fort was on top of a hill, and there were steps all

the way down to the road below. Halfway down, Neil dialled Shefali's number. She picked up on the fourth ring.

'Hi,' she said cheerfully.

At the sound of her voice Neil felt his pulse begin to race. 'Hi,' he said softly. 'You doing OK?'

At the other end of the line Shefali was sorely tempted to yell that she wasn't. What did he expect, after walking out on her like that last night? But better sense prevailed, and she said instead, 'I'm good. How's the shoot going?'

Neil grimaced. 'As well as can be expected, I guess. This whole recreating history bit isn't my kind of thing. Rafiq's managing it. I'm just standing in front of the camera and saying my lines.'

Shefali had spent the afternoon watching clips of his earlier shows on the internet. She could picture him, standing in front of the fort in his trademark white T-shirt and faded jeans, his hair ruffled by the breeze and the sun glinting off his grey-blue eyes. She shut her eyes for a second. *Short fling*, she said to herself. *That's all—don't start getting obsessed with him*. Aloud she said, 'Has your fan club followed you?' He'd been complaining about a bunch of college girls who'd taken to haunting his shoots, giggling and simpering just out of camera range and making a regular nuisance of themselves.

'Rafiq offered them roles as handmaidens to the queen,' Neil said. 'They're running around somewhere in *ghaghra cholis*—I think Rafiq's their new hero.'

'Right,' Shefali said, and there was a pause.

'We need to talk,' Neil said abruptly.

Shefali tensed. It didn't sound as if he was going to tell her he wanted to spend the rest of his life with her.

'Over the phone?' she asked carefully.

She could hear the reluctance in his voice when he replied, 'No, I guess not. Are you free to meet this evening?'

'I've got to go out to for dinner with some of the teachers,' Shefali said. 'What about tomorrow? It's Saturday, and I don't have much to do much other than paperwork for the school.'

'I'm at this shoot all day,' Neil said. 'Do you want to meet me here? We can do a picnic lunch somewhere near the fort.'

Shefali made a face. A picnic lunch sounded OK in theory, but—having seen Neil at work on two previous occasions—she knew she'd be kept hanging around like a spare wheel while he dealt with the dozens of problems that cropped up.

'No,' she said. 'It's too hot for a picnic. Would you like to come over for dinner instead?' The second she said it, she realised she'd made a false move—he'd assume she wanted to continue where they'd stopped the night before. Her hunch was confirmed a second later.

'I don't think that's a good idea,' he said. 'Are you free now? I can take the rest of the day off.'

To say that Rafiq wasn't pleased was an understatement—he was livid.

'You can't just walk off,' he stormed at Neil. 'It's taken me *hours* to get everything just right, and the light's perfect, and *now* you announce you need to go. Where's the fire?'

'There's something I need to take care of,' Neil said, wishing he'd lied and said he wasn't feeling well.

'*What* do you need to take care of?' Rafiq bellowed. 'Why now? Why can't it wait?'

'Leave him alone, Rafiq,' Priti intervened. 'We can do the scenes without him today and the rest tomorrow—it'd be easier, actually. He's looking like hell, anyway—look at the circles under his eyes.'

'What do you expect if he spends the night seducing village maidens instead of getting his beauty sleep?' Rafiq muttered sulkily. Neil made a sudden movement, and Rafiq's eyes widened in alarm. 'Chill, man...I'm just saying,' he protested. 'I've no *idea* what you've been doing—though, given the way you're behaving, I can guess,' he added under his breath.

As Neil swung away Priti gave Rafiq an affectionate punch on the arm. 'Come on, let's get the show going. Oh, and the last time I checked Neil's still our boss. He doesn't need our permission if he wants to take the afternoon off.'

'I'm glad someone remembers that,' Neil called over his shoulder as he headed down the stairs.

Rafiq yelled back, 'Yeah, right—pull rank on your old friends.' He was frowning when he turned back to Priti. 'It's that girl who runs Nina's school. I didn't think she'd be his type.'

Priti shrugged. 'It's none of our business. And it's a relief he's getting mixed up with a normal girl his own age rather than those harpies he sleeps with in Mumbai.'

Twenty minutes later Neil was sitting next to Shefali on a bench in a public park in the middle of the city. She'd refused to meet at a coffee shop, and he didn't want to go to her flat. The park seemed the most neutral place to meet, where they could talk without being overheard.

'I don't see what you're so worked up about,' Shefali

was saying. Her tone was exasperated, but inside she was a bundle of nerves.

'It feels like I took advantage of you on the rebound!' he said. 'I've had affairs before, but they were with women who—well, who knew their way around. You're not like that.'

'I'm the kind men take home to meet their mother? Is that it?' Shefali asked, but he looked away, not replying.

Odd how something that she'd normally have taken as a compliment was making her heart sink into her shoes. She'd spent the morning agonising over Neil's evident reluctance to take their relationship any further, and while she was no closer to figuring out her own feelings for him she knew she couldn't let him go. Not yet.

'I don't want a serious relationship either,' she said finally, thinking furiously. Perhaps that would make him stay—at least long enough for her to get over the worst of this infatuation that had her writhing helplessly in its grip. And it had the added advantage of being almost true.

Neil turned to look at her in surprise. 'You don't?'

She shrugged. 'You're right about the rebound thing,' she said, trying to keep her voice light and casual. 'I'm not ready for a new relationship yet. But I do think I deserve some fun.'

There—she'd said it. It hadn't come out sounding quite right—'fun' seemed to put Neil on par with carnival rides and ice cream on a summer day—but his implacable expression was relaxing a little, so she continued.

'I need to prove to myself that I can manage perfectly

well on my own. I don't *want* to be rid of one loser of a guy just to get shackled to another.'

'Thanks,' he said drily, but he was smiling.

Shefali felt her heart give a happy little skip inside her chest. She flapped a hand at him. 'You know what I mean. You're not a loser—if anything, you're a bit of a role model for me.'

Neil did an almost visible double-take. 'Role model in what way, exactly?'

Shefali leaned forward, taking his hand eagerly. 'Don't you see? Your life was a mess too, after Reema left, and your parents and sister wanted to take over, but you managed on your own. And you did brilliantly! Look at you now—you're successful in your career and Nina's perfect. She's intelligent, and cute, and she adores you. So as far as I'm concerned you're a role model.' She pulled a face. 'Though in my case it's not a kid I need to bring up properly, it's myself. To make up for all the years I was wafting around in training to be the perfect wife.'

She held her breath as she watched Neil absorb what she'd just said. He looked half convinced, and hopefully he wouldn't enquire into her motives too closely. Being a diplomat's daughter had its advantages—she knew exactly when to stop laying it on.

'What're you suggesting, then?'

She heaved a sigh of relief. The rest was going to be easy. At least she'd have him for a little while longer. And hopefully she'd manage to get over him afterwards. She touched his hand gently.

'We keep on seeing each other. For as long as you're in town. When you leave, we say goodbye—and we part with no regrets on either side.'

'Why would you want something like that?' Neil asked, his eyes troubled.

Shefali stifled a sigh of exasperation. That was the trouble with Neil, she thought. In spite of the sexy man-of-the-world exterior, he was just so damn *nice* inside. Most men would have jumped at the suggestion of a short, no-strings-attached fling. Neil wanted to be sure that he didn't end up hurting her by mistake.

She gave him a brief smile. 'I just told you—a serious relationship's not something I can deal with right now. But I do want to live life a little. I've never dated, never had a boyfriend, never stayed up the whole night dancing, never really had much fun. That's all I want out of this. And, if you don't mind my saying, I think it'd do you some good as well.'

Neil scanned her face, searching for a clue towards how she really felt. Something about what she was saying didn't ring true. He was incredibly tempted, though—the years since Nina was born had been completely devoid of anything remotely resembling fun with the opposite sex. He'd had a few relationships, but those had been discreet liaisons of convenience with older women, nothing that made him feel young and alive like Shefali did.

'I'm not typical boyfriend material,' he warned finally. 'And I don't think this is the kind of place you can stay up the whole night dancing.'

'I'm sure we can think of something else to do all night long,' she said huskily.

Neil's senses immediately sprang to high alert. The effect she had on him was incredible—even Reema hadn't been able to set him on fire with a single word or a touch the way Shefali could.

Knowing that he was allowing himself to be talked into this, he took her hand and looked into her beautiful brown eyes. 'An offer I can't refuse,' he said, with a rueful smile tugging at the corners of his perfectly shaped mouth. 'My head keeps telling me that we're making a mistake, but I'm only here for a few weeks more, and once I'm back in Mumbai...'

He'd meant to say that they wouldn't be able to meet very often if they were in different cities, but Shefali assumed he was about to add another set of caveats.

'It'll be over when you leave,' she said, breaking in before he could say anything more. 'I understand that, and it's fine.'

She slid her hands slowly up his chest and finally Neil's self-control snapped. His arms came around to clasp her roughly, and his lips were hot and impatient against hers.

CHAPTER SIX

THE NEXT TWO months were probably the most fulfilling and the most frustrating of Shefali's life. Fulfilling because she spent every long, passion-filled night in Neil's arms, and frustrating because he was so clearly unprepared to give her anything more than a few weeks of mind-blowing sex.

She couldn't blame him—that was what she'd agreed to—and she even felt a little guilty, expecting more. But she'd become addicted to Neil's night-time visits—although she'd been very careful to hide the extent to which she was involved. Even to herself she didn't admit quite how close she was to falling in love with Neil. And she wasn't sure how long she could keep up the charade. Or if she even wanted to keep it up. It would be far more honest to tell Neil that she couldn't do this any more, that she wasn't the kind of person who could handle a fling without getting emotionally involved. A civilised break would be the best thing for both of them. Her heart quailed at thought of quite so much honesty, though. It was all very well rehearsing the lines in her head, but actually saying them to Neil would be humiliating for her and embarrassing for him.

She glanced at Neil, sleeping beside her, an arm casually draped across her waist. He had no inkling of the doubts she was struggling with—he probably thought that the arrangement was working out perfectly. Sighing, she looked at the clock on the bedside table. It was almost five—it would be dawn in another half an hour.

'You need to go,' she whispered into Neil's ear, and he turned, pulling her into his arms and nuzzling the sensitive skin at the base of her throat. 'Neil, don't!' she gasped as his mouth wandered lower, and he pulled away regretfully.

She was right—he did need to leave, and the walk back to his house was a longish one. It was still dark outside, but that was the whole point—he didn't want people knowing that he was spending nights at Shefali's flat.

'How much longer do you think you guys will need to complete filming?' Shefali asked as she watched Neil pull on his jeans and T-shirt.

'I think we'll be done in a week,' Neil said, and Shefali's heart sank. Just one more week. She gave Neil a quick look. He seemed entirely unaffected by the fact that they wouldn't see each other again after next week—from his expression they might have been talking about the government's fiscal deficit.

'Back to Mumbai after that, then?' she said lightly.

Neil nodded, and came to sit next to her on the bed. 'We'll be in touch,' he said, taking her hand and gently running his finger down her wrist. He would miss her unbearably, though he was careful not to let her see that. Sober thought had made him come to the conclusion that a short fling would be the best for both of them. But he still couldn't help saying, 'Maybe you could come and see us in Mumbai some time?'

'The way I come and see you now?' Shefali asked
sarcastically, jerking her hand away from his. Ever since
they'd got into this physical relationship they'd stopped
meeting during the day—Neil had even stopped coming to school to pick up Nina. She'd tried not to be upset
by the fact that he didn't want to see her outside of bed,
but it was difficult not to feel hurt.

Neil's eyebrows flew up at her tone. 'You're welcome
to come and see me whenever you want,' he said, though
he knew it wasn't true. He hadn't expressly told her *not*
to come near him during the day, but the message had
been pretty loud and clear.

'Right,' she said. 'As long as I wear a veil and cover
my face?'

'I don't know why you're choosing to get upset about
this—' Neil began.

Shefali cut in quickly. 'Because I feel like I'm your
mistress,' she said angrily. 'I know we said it wasn't
going to be serious, but I hate sneaking around.'

'We discussed it,' Neil replied. 'This is still a fairly
conservative city. You're running a playschool—it
wouldn't do you much good if word got around that
you were sleeping with me.'

'That doesn't explain why we don't meet in other
ways,' she flared at him. 'With the guys from your crew,
or with the teachers from the school. We're supposed to
be friends, but the only reason we meet is to sleep together.' She didn't say it, but what hurt the most was the
way he'd tried to keep her away from Nina. Of course
Nina still came to school every day, but not once had
Neil suggested even a visit to the park together. Feeling
a bit like a scarlet woman, insisting on being accepted

by her lover's family, she said, 'You didn't even come across and say hello on Sports Day.'

'I wasn't sure if we'd be able to keep up the act in front of so many people,' Neil said wearily. 'Believe me, I'm not trying to avoid you. I'm just trying to make sure that it doesn't get embarrassing for you when I leave.'

It was the tone that finally decided her. Already Neil was beginning to sound as if he was tired of her—and it had been only two months since the night he'd stayed over for the first time. If she dragged this on any further she'd end up hating herself.

'Right, then, maybe we should stop seeing each other altogether?' she said curtly. 'I thought this would be fun, but it isn't. It's cheap and sordid and I've had enough.'

Neil stayed silent. Warring thoughts flew through his mind. He'd grown to care for Shefali a lot more than he liked to admit, and the thought of not seeing her any more caused a physical pain in the region of his heart. But then there was Nina to think of, and Shefali herself. Nina was surprisingly mature for her age, and she'd already asked him a couple of times if he planned to marry again. And as for Shefali, asking her to enter into any kind of long-term relationship was unfair, given the amount of baggage he came with.

He turned to Shefali to tell her so, but the sight of tears trembling on her long lashes stopped him. He'd never seen her cry before—she'd lost her temper often, but she'd never cried. Not even when she was telling him about her broken engagement, or her estrangement from her parents. Even now she was blinking the tears back and glaring at him. With a muttered curse, Neil gathered her into his arms, tightening his hold when she resisted. For a while she continued to struggle, pushing at his chest with her hands, but then she quietened down, resting her head against his shoulder.

'It's Nina, isn't it?' she asked softly after a while, without looking up.

'Partly,' Neil said. 'She's fond of you, but I don't know how she'd react if she knew we were dating. I don't even know if she's old enough to understand what dating is—she might just assume that we're going to get married. I know it's not fair to you, but...' He struggled for words.

'But she's your daughter,' Shefali said, freeing herself from his arms and sitting up. 'She'll always come first with you—I understand that. But you can't shut yourself off from women for your entire life, can you? You're only twenty-eight. Don't you want to marry again? Have a regular life?' She added hastily, in case he misunderstood, 'I don't mean with me—we always meant this to be a short-term thing—but with someone else?'

Neil stood up and went to window. 'I've thought about it a fair bit,' he said. 'I don't want to remarry. There's no guarantee it would work out this time, and it would be horribly unfair to Nina if it didn't. And there might be more children—that's something I most definitely don't want.'

Reema had done a thorough job on him, Shefali thought, looking at Neil's rigid back. He was so closed to the idea of a permanent relationship it was as if commitment had been surgically removed from his psyche.

As another thought struck Shefali, she said, 'Do you think Reema will ever...'

He was shaking his head already. 'Reema won't

come back. And I don't want her to in any case—I've wasted enough years of my life on her.' At Shefali's puzzled look, he said wryly, 'We started dating at sixteen—we'd been together for seven years when Nina came along.'

Seven years! No wonder he was taking so long to get over her. And what kind of parents allowed their children to start dating seriously at sixteen? Shefali could feel the disapproval showing in her face.

Neil smiled. 'I know,' he said. 'But things are little different in Kolkata, and our families were close, so we used to spend a lot of time together even before we started dating. Anyway, that's beside the point.' He came back from the window to kneel by the side of the bed, taking both her hands in his. 'I don't want you thinking that I'm ashamed of being with you,' he said. 'I was trying to protect Nina—and myself—but I wasn't thinking straight.'

He looked so contrite that Shefali couldn't help smiling. 'You could give me some credit for maturity,' she suggested. 'I won't automatically leap into your arms if you come and speak to me in public.'

'I know,' he said. 'I'm more worried about my own reaction.'

He turned her hands over and pressed his lips to each palm. It was a gesture that never failed to send tingles down her spine, and she almost missed what he said when he started speaking again. Freeing her hands, she started listening more carefully.

'This might sound a little weird, but why don't you come home for dinner tonight? Nina's been pestering me for ages to ask you over, and Bela Mashi's an excellent cook. She'll jump at the chance of trying out some of her fancier dishes.'

'So you're asking me over to make Nina and Bela Mashi happy? Is that it?' Shefali asked, only half teasingly.

'Of course,' Neil said, laughing up at her. 'They're the two most important women in my life.'

Which was probably nothing but the plain, unvarnished truth, Shefali thought, but she leaned over and kissed him hard on the lips. 'I'll check my calendar,' she said. 'Just in case I have a hot date that I've forgotten about.'

It was almost six when Neil finally left, and Shefali closed the door behind him and got into the shower. The cold spray stung against her skin, but it helped clear her head. She needed to be realistic. An invitation to dinner didn't change the fact that Neil would be leaving in a week. And she was coming closer and closer to falling in love with him, despite knowing that he wasn't in the least bit in love with her. A clean break would be best, however much it hurt, rather than kidding herself that something might come of their relationship.

Her conviction that getting involved with Neil had been a mistake was further strengthened when Deepa, one of the younger teachers at the school, took her aside during the lunch break.

'What's the matter?' Shefali asked, a little irritated at being disturbed when she had work to do.

Deepa flushed. 'My brother's on the night shift at the factory,' she said, almost stammering with nervousness. 'He passes the school on his way home from work, and today he said he saw a man leaving the building at around six in the morning.'

'So?' Shefali asked brusquely.

'He won't tell anyone, but he recognised Nina's dad. If anyone else sees him they'll talk…' She saw the expression on Shefali's face and hurried on, 'I know it's none of my business, but this is a small town. People gossip a lot. You're new here, and you live alone. It could get unpleasant. I was worried, so I thought I'd just tell you…'

She was babbling in her nervousness, and Shefali took pity on her. Deepa was a timid girl to begin with, and it couldn't have been easy, nerving herself to speak to her boss on such a touchy topic.

'Thanks for telling me,' she said quietly. 'You don't need to worry, Deepa, Neil will be leaving town for good next week.'

Deepa looked so relieved that Shefali smiled involuntarily—a Victorian miss would have probably reacted in a similar way on being told that Jack the Ripper was leaving London. One of Deepa's charges came dancing out into the corridor, distracting her, and Shefali was free to go back to her office.

Neil had invited Rafiq and Priti for dinner as well. Shefali wasn't sure whether that was to avoid being alone with her, or to prove to her that he wasn't trying to keep her a guilty secret. Rafiq had offered to pick her up on his way to Neil's house and she accepted, not wanting to ruin her hair in an auto.

'Wow,' Rafiq said, clearly impressed when she got into the car.

She'd dressed simply, in a sleeveless white Lucknowi *churidaar kameez*. The *kameez* was covered in white *chikankari* embroidery, and she'd thrown a blue printed silk *dupatta* over her shoulders. Her eyes were outlined in *kohl*, but she'd used only the slightest hint of lipgloss. Her hair fell loose over her shoulders. Her jewellery was dramatic—a silver choker with uneven pieces of lapis set into it, matching dangly earrings and a silver cuff bracelet around one wrist.

Priti, who was also in the car, leaned across to examine the bracelet more closely. 'Very pretty,' she pronounced. 'You get really good jewellery in Delhi—not like the expensive junk they have in Mumbai.'

Shefali smiled. Her mother had wanted her to get rid of all her silver jewellery before she got married— 'Only gold and diamonds once you're married. There's always platinum or white gold if you want. Silver looks so tacky!' That was one argument Shefali had won, and she'd brought her favourite silver pieces with her to Jabalpur. The heavy gold jewellery that had been bought for her wedding was locked in a safe in Delhi, and she didn't care if she never saw it again.

Nina was hopping on one foot with excitement when they arrived, and she flung her arms around Shefali as soon she stepped into the house. Neil gave her a wry look. 'She's been over the moon ever since she found out you were coming over,' he said.

'No such welcome for me, eh?' Rafiq demanded, giving Nina a ferocious look.

She giggled happily and darted away as he tried to grab her, coming up to say hello only after Neil said something stern in Bengali.

'I didn't realise you spoke Bengali at home,' Priti remarked.

Neil shrugged. 'Bengali dad, grew up in Kolkata,

married a Bengali—I didn't really have much of a choice,' he said. 'Wine or beer?'

Shefali opted for wine, but the evening was already a little spoilt for her by his reference to his ex-wife. Among friends he obviously spoke about her quite casually, and it wasn't surprising—with Nina around it was unlikely they'd forget that he'd been married. She was distracted by Bela Mashi, hurrying into the room, beaming from ear to ear.

'My favourite woman in the entire world,' Rafiq said in Hindi, and jumped up to hug Bela.

She pushed him off, pretending to be upset, but obviously hugely pleased. 'What nonsense you talk,' she said in heavily accented Hindi.

'And what nonsense your Hindi is,' Rafiq retorted. 'Bela Mashi, when will you learn that Bengali doesn't automatically become Hindi if you speak at twice the volume and half the speed?'

'I've managed fine till now,' Bela Mashi said indignantly, reverting to English. 'No one in this God-forsaken city understands Bengali—how d'you think I run the house if I can't speak Hindi?' She turned to Shefali and gave her a big smile. 'So nice to see you, Shefali *didi*. Nina's been so excited.'

Bela's English, with its part-Bengali, part-British accent, had come as a surprise to Shefali when they'd first met, but now it made sense—Neil's British mother would naturally have hired an English-speaking nanny, and over the years her accent must have rubbed off on Bela. It would be interesting to speak to Neil's mother and figure out if the reverse had happened as well.

'Dinner's ready, if you want to eat,' Bela was saying.

They had just got up to go to the dining room when

Shefali's phone rang. She went back to retrieve it, frowning at the unfamiliar number. The voice on the other end wasn't unfamiliar, though, and Neil turned around sharply when she said, 'Pranav!'

'Yes, it's me,' Pranav said. 'Don't hang up, Shefali.'

'I'm not planning to,' she said grimly. 'Whatever you have to say, Pranav, I'm sure it'll be interesting.'

Neil was still hovering at the doorway, a concerned look on his face, but Shefali waved him away. This was one conversation she didn't want anyone overhearing. She waited till she could hear him in the dining room, making excuses for her, and then she said into the phone, 'Go on.'

'I didn't realise you'd left Delhi,' Pranav said. 'I tried your old number a few times once things had settled down a little, but I couldn't get through. And your parents weren't willing to talk to me. I finally managed to get your number through a friend.'

'Congratulations,' Shefali said. 'And now that you do finally have my number, can you hurry up and tell me what you want? I'm at someone's home for dinner.'

It had been only a few months, but it already felt as if Pranav was a stranger—part of a life she'd left behind a long while ago. In fact he always had been a stranger—it was just that she was admitting it to herself for the first time. She didn't even feel as angry with him as she'd thought she would. She just wanted him to say what he had to and get out of her life.

'I wanted to apologise,' he said after a brief pause. 'I don't have any excuses for the way I treated you, and I don't expect you to forgive me. I can only say I'm sorry.'

'Right,' Shefali said, thinking back to the nightmare

of the wedding he'd failed to turn up for. *Sorry* didn't even begin to cover it.

'I know you've left home,' he said. 'And that your parents weren't too…umm…supportive. If you need anything—'

'I'm fine,' Shefali cut in, suppressing a second's urge to burst into hysterical giggles. What on earth was he planning to offer her? Money? Emotional support? A place to stay?

'My parents aren't too thrilled with me either,' he said. 'Dad's cut off ties completely, so I'm no longer working for him. Actually, I'm living off Priya right now—until I get a job.'

So he wasn't offering money, then? Unless his girlfriend was planning to sponsor him out of his guilt trip. The conversation was turning out to be a lot less difficult then she'd thought.

'I'm sure things will work out,' she said, not even bothering to sound as if she meant it. 'Maybe your father will come around once you two are married?'

'We hope so too,' Pranav said. 'I only wish I'd mustered up the guts to stand up to him a lot earlier. It would have saved you all the trouble and embarrassment I put you through.'

'At least you figured things out before we ended up married to each other,' Shefali said. There was a brief pause. 'I need to go now, Pranav. Everyone's waiting for me.'

'Can we meet when you're back in Delhi?' Pranav asked. 'I'd like to introduce Priya to you.'

'I'll let you know when I'm there next,' Shefali said, though she had no intention of doing anything of the sort.

She was pretty amazed at her own powers of self-control—she'd managed to complete the conversation without losing her temper or even raising her voice. That had to be some kind of world record for a woman left hanging at the altar with no word of explanation. But, to her surprise, she didn't even feel angry with Pranav any more. The only feeling she could dredge up was a kind of weary contempt for his lack of courage and her own gullibility.

'All OK?' Neil asked in an undertone as she rejoined the others.

She nodded. 'I'm fine,' she said, for the second time in the evening, and realised she meant it. The chapter with Pranav was closed, and it was time to move on. With or without Neil by her side.

'Will you have some chicken?' Bela Mashi asked, and Shefali looked up with a start. It seemed very prosaic to be bothering about food at a time like this, but she found that she was very hungry. Not surprising, given that her lunch had consisted of a single banana and a glass of juice.

'Thanks,' she said as Bela heaped her plate with rice and chicken curry. 'This is good,' she said, taking a spoonful.

Rafiq grinned. 'Bela Mashi's the best cook in the universe,' he said. 'I suppose *you* can cook, but for a bachelor klutz like me she's a life-saver.'

Shefali laughed. 'I can cook,' she said. 'It's all the chopping and cleaning up that I can't handle. I'm too used to someone else doing it for me.'

'Come over for a meal whenever you like,' Bela said generously.

'Yes, teacher,' Nina chimed in. 'It's so nice to have

you here! It gets boring with just Dad and Bela Mashi around.'

'I doubt she'll be free to come and entertain you very often, Nina,' Neil said. 'And we'll be leaving in a week anyway.'

His voice was light, but there was an undercurrent of strain, and he avoided catching Shefali's eye. Her heart plummeted at his tone. Evidently the dinner invitation hadn't been more than a sop. He had no intention of letting her get any closer to his family. Her temporary sense of well-being evaporated, and she was left staring miserably at the mound of food on her plate.

Conscious of Rafiq's and Priti's curious eyes on her, she plastered a bright smile on her face and said, 'I'll need to ask Bela Mashi for a few recipes, I see! Her cooking's out of this world.'

Neil had opened his mouth to say something, but he shut it again as Rafiq started pulling Bela's leg unmercifully. He'd reacted to Nina's remark without thinking, and he knew he'd upset Shefali. But there was very little he could do to set things right without publicly acknowledging their relationship, and he wasn't ready for that particular step just yet. Perhaps he never would be.

Turning his attention from Shefali to Nina, he felt his tensed muscles relax. Whatever his feelings about Shefali might be, Nina was his priority and always would be. The rest of his life would have to fit around what was best for *her*, and if some of the decisions he needed to take were tough he'd have to live with them.

CHAPTER SEVEN

SHEFALI SLAMMED A file shut with a thud. 'The admissions records are in a mess,' she said. 'Why aren't they filed by class, rather than this way?'

'Mrs Dubey always wanted them to be in alphabetical order,' the teacher in front of her said stolidly. 'She said she found it easier that way.'

'Yes, but—' Shefali started to answer in exasperation, but broke off as her mobile phone started ringing.

She swivelled her chair around and picked up the phone to glance at the display. Neil. Her heart began to race and she nodded to the teacher, who picked up the file and sailed majestically and very slowly out of her office. Only when the door had shut behind her did Shefali take the call.

'Hi,' she said carefully, trying to keep her voice as calm and neutral as possible, though her heart was now bouncing around in her chest like a high-school cheerleader.

'I need your help,' Neil said without preamble.

'Is everything OK?' Shefali asked quickly, alerted by the strained tone of his voice.

'Not really. Bela Mashi's fallen and broken her ankle. She's in bad shape. It's a multiple fracture. I need to stay at the hospital with her until the doctors figure out what to do. Can you keep Nina with you until I can come and fetch her?'

'Yes, of course,' Shefali said. 'I'll take her to my flat after school. Do you want me to tell her what's happened?'

Neil hesitated. 'Maybe you should—but play it down. She's very attached to Bela Mashi.'

Bela had been Neil's nanny as well, Shefali remembered—he was probably as attached to her as Nina was. And a multiple fracture at her age sounded dangerous. No wonder he was sounding so stressed.

'Take care,' she said softly, but Neil had already hung up.

There was no point getting Nina out of class, so Shefali waited till the last class finished at twelve-thirty.

'Can you close up here?' she asked one of the other teachers. 'I need to tell Nina something.'

Nina took the news calmly, only asking if she could go to the hospital and visit Bela.

'I'm sure you can,' Shefali said. 'But we'll have to wait for your dad to call back and tell us how she is before we plan a visit. In the meantime, let's figure out what we can give you for lunch.'

'Peanut butter sandwich?' Nina asked hopefully.

Shefali shook her head. 'Sorry, you're out of luck,' she said. 'No peanut butter. You can have a jam sandwich—or you can have *roti* and vegetables with me.'

Looking disappointed, Nina opted for the jam sandwich, and Shefali made one for her, removing the crusts carefully as Nina looked on.

'Here you go,' she said, handing Nina the sandwich on a plate. Once she was done, Shefali tucked her in for a nap, and went back to the dining room to finish her own lunch. Neil didn't call, and Shefali was just starting to worry when the doorbell rang.

Neil was standing on the doorstep, a small pink rucksack in his hand. He looked tired, and worried, and Shefali's heart went out to him.

'How's she doing?' she asked.

Neil shook his head. 'She's in a lot of pain,' he said. 'They'll need to insert pins to hold the bone back together. It'll take her a while to recover. Thank heavens I was at home when it happened—she wouldn't even have been able to get to a phone.'

'Sit down and I'll get you some tea,' Shefali said soothingly.

'I can't stay,' Neil said. 'I just came by to drop some of Nina's things off. I need to get back to the hospital right away.'

'What about the shoot?' Shefali asked.

'Cancelled for the next few days. I've asked Rafiq to see if we can manage with the footage we already have—if we can't I'll try and wrap it up in a couple of days once everything is under control.'

'Nina's asleep,' Shefali said. 'Do you want to come in and see her?'

Neil hesitated, and then followed her in. Nina was curled up in the corner of the living room settee, covered with a light wrap of Shefali's. Her feet were sticking out from under the wrap, and Shefali leaned across to cover them.

'No, don't,' Neil said quickly. 'She doesn't like her feet being covered.'

Shefali smiled, and put the wrap back the way it had been. Neil was looking at his daughter, the expression on his face so tender that it brought a lump to Shefali's throat.

'I hate bothering you like this,' Neil said as he walked back towards the door. 'But there's no one else she'd be OK with—except Priti and Rafiq, maybe, but they don't have any experience with kids.'

'And they'd be busy working,' Shefali said. 'Don't worry, Neil. She can stay here as long as she likes.' She hesitated a little. 'It's fun having her around—I always miss the kids terribly when they go home after school and I'm left here all alone.'

He smiled briefly, but there was a wary look in his eyes that made her think she shouldn't have said so much.

Striving for a more practical note, she continued, 'Only next time you come by bring me a jar of peanut butter—she wasn't too happy with the jam sandwiches I gave her for lunch.'

Neil unzipped the pink rucksack and put a jar on the table. 'I figured you'd need it,' he said. 'Normally we only let her have it for breakfast, but I guess you can make an exception now.'

'I'll try and make sure she has some rice and vegetables too,' Shefali promised. 'And, Neil…?' He stopped at the door and looked back at her. 'Don't look so worried,' she said softly, putting up a hand to touch his face lightly. 'Everything will be OK.'

Neil's hand came up to grip hers, and he pressed a swift kiss into her palm. 'I hope so,' he said. 'And thanks for looking after Nina. I don't know what I'd have done without you.'

Shefali watched Neil run down the stairs and get into his car. Her palm still tingled where he'd kissed it, but the tingle reached her cheeks when she turned around and realised that Nina was watching her with a wide, unblinking stare. She was about to launch into an explanation suitable for a four-year-old when Nina shut her eyes and went back to sleep. Shefali heaved a sigh of relief. If she was lucky Nina wouldn't remember anything when she woke up.

For the next couple of days she hardly saw Neil, though Nina was with her constantly. She was a low-maintenance child, keeping herself busy with colouring books and a set of blocks, and she had a doll that she carried around with her everywhere she went. If there were other kids around she played with them, otherwise she seemed just as happy on her own. Shefali had lost her heart to Nina before the end of their first day together, but she took care to conceal the fact. Nina was still a pupil, and openly showing that she liked her more than the other kids wouldn't be fair. Also, Neil might misunderstand her motives—it was safer to be briskly affectionate with Nina, the way she was with all her other students.

On the fourth day after her fall, Bela Mashi was allowed to come home from hospital. 'Such a fuss about nothing,' she grumbled when Shefali went to visit her. Her ankle and half her leg was in a cast, and Neil had employed a nurse to help her get around—something that Bela resented fiercely.

'Bela Mashi was convinced her leg would fix itself if she rubbed some Iodex on it and lay down for an hour,' Neil said.

Bela glared at him. 'That was before I knew it was

broken,' she said in exaggeratedly patient tones. 'Once I knew it was broken I didn't fuss, did I?'

'No, it was the doctors who fussed, poor things, once they figured out what a scary old woman you are,' Neil retorted. Then his gaze softened. 'I'm glad you're back,' he said quietly.

Bela sniffed, hugely pleased but doing her best not to show it. 'Much good I am, lying around with my leg in plaster,' she said. 'How you're planning to manage Nina, I don't know.'

As if on cue, Neil's phone rang, and he fished it out of his jacket pocket.

'My mother,' he mouthed to Shefali, and she tried hard not to eavesdrop as Neil started filling his mother in on Bela's condition.

Bela looked hopefully at Neil. 'Ask her if she can come,' she said. 'Nina hasn't seen her for a long while, and she'll be able to take care of her while you work.'

Neil nodded. 'If you could,' he was saying into the phone. 'Nina's with Shefali now—you remember I told you about her—but I can't impose.'

Torn between happiness that he'd actually talked about her to his mother, and the fact that he was about to remove the only link between them, Shefali protested, 'It's not a problem—she can stay as long as she needs to.'

At the other end of the phone, Barbara Mitra frowned. She knew her son well, and he wouldn't trust Nina with anyone unless he had implicit faith in them. And he'd known Shefali for only a few weeks... Hoping she was making the right decision, she said briskly 'I'd love to come down, Neil, but this isn't a very good time for me, I'm afraid. We've got interior decorators doing up the house, and your father needs to travel. I don't see how I can shut things up and come over.'

'Right...' Neil said slowly. Over the years since Nina was born he'd got so used to fending off offers of help from his mother and sister that he wasn't prepared for the help *not* being forthcoming when he actually needed it.

'And Anita's in Sri Lanka,' his mother was saying. 'Otherwise I'm sure she'd have offered to take Nina.'

She'd have thought of an excuse as well, most probably, Neil thought uncharitably of his older sister. Well, it looked as if he was on his own, then.

'Do you want to speak to Bela Mashi?' he said aloud, and when his mother said she did, he passed the phone to Bela.

'No good,' he said to Shefali gloomily. 'She can't come down, and Bela Mashi can't be moved for another two weeks at least. I guess I don't have a choice—I'll tell Rafiq and the crew to head back to Mumbai, and I'll stay on here.'

Two more weeks of having Neil around! Disgusted with the way her heart leapt with excitement at the thought, Shefali said as dispassionately as possible, 'Isn't there any other solution? If you have to work in Mumbai you could take Nina and go. Bela Mashi should be OK with a full-time nurse, and I'm here if she needs help.'

Neil shook his head. 'I wouldn't be able to work even if I went back. There's no one else I could leave Nina with.'

Bela Mashi had finished talking, and she beckoned Neil over to hand him his mobile. 'You'll have to take Nina to buy new clothes for Durga Pujo,' she said. 'And you'll need to get stuff for the house as well. With all this going on I'd clean forgotten that the festival's around the corner until your mother mentioned it.'

Durga Puja was a big festival in the part of the country Bela came from, and she'd made a point of keeping up the Mitra family tradition by celebrating it with Nina wherever they were. Before she'd broken her ankle she'd already found out that there was a large Bengali community in the city—she'd even identified the two big *pandals* she wanted to take Nina to.

Neil's brow puckered with worry. 'Maybe we should let it go this year?' he suggested. 'I have my hands full anyway, and I don't know the first thing about Pujo shopping.'

'Shefali will help you,' Bela Mashi said firmly. 'You can't *not* celebrate the festival. It's just not done. It'll bring bad luck to the family.'

Neil groaned. The most rational of people normally, Bela tended to go off at the deep end whenever he questioned any of her pet traditions. Also, she was quite capable of trying to get up and go to the shops herself if he didn't agree to go. Risking permanent disability was small stuff compared to bringing bad luck to the family.

'I'll leave you to discuss it,' Shefali said, standing up hastily. 'I'll just say goodbye to Nina and let myself out.'

As she left the room she heard the conversation switch to Bengali—whenever Bela was in fighting mode her English deserted her.

Nina was tucking her favourite doll into bed, carefully smoothing down its matted nylon hair.

'Dora needs a haircut, doesn't she?' Shefali asked, kneeling down next to Nina.

Nina was shaking her head, however. 'She's a *jungli*

Dora,' she explained. 'My other dolls have proper hair—
I don't play with them much.'

'Won't Dora feel bad, then, if the other dolls have
better hair?'

Nina looked at her as if she was mad. 'Dora isn't
real,' she explained patiently. 'She doesn't feel things.'

'Right,' Shefali said. 'Lucky Dora.' Lucky in many
ways, actually—think of the amount of money she
would be saving on product and conditioner. And not
being able to feel things—that was a pretty handy trait
to have too. 'I'll see you around, Nina,' Shefali said.
'I'm going back home now.'

Nina looked up immediately, her eyes registering
dismay. 'Don't go so soon!' she said. 'I thought you'd
stay for dinner with us.'

Shefali shook her head. Nina's eyes *were* like Neil's.
Not in size and colour, maybe, but the expression in
them was so like Neil's it was uncanny. There was no
way Neil would look so upset at the thought of her leaving for home, though—he was probably dying to see
her on her way.

Or maybe not.

Getting the distinct feeling that she was being
watched, she swung around to see Neil leaning against
the doorjamb. He was smiling at her, and this time the
smile reached his eyes fully.

'How d'you feel about helping us with a spot of Pujo
shopping?' he asked.

Shefali found herself feeling so ridiculously pleased
that he wanted to spend more time with her that she had
to fight to keep a goofy grin off her face.

'Lost the argument, I see,' she said.

He shrugged. 'Bela Mashi has known me since I was

born. When she's serious about getting her way I don't stand a chance.' He looked across at Nina. 'Go and get ready, munchkin, we leave in ten minutes.'

Nina sprang up with a little squeal and rushed off in the direction of her room, and Neil came in further to stand next to Shefali. Still kneeling on the ground, Shefali found herself at a distinct disadvantage—he towered over her, and close-up the aura of raw masculinity he exuded was overpowering. A second later, however, he had hunkered down next to her to look at the doll she was mechanically patting.

Neil stretched out a hand and touched the doll lightly. 'I see you've met my granddaughter,' he said wryly. 'I hope she's been saying good things about me.'

'She's not real,' Shefali informed him. 'She can't feel things, apparently.'

'Hmm,' Neil said. 'Did Nina tell you that?'

Shefali nodded, hardly daring to breathe as Neil got to his feet, taking her hands and gently pulling her up to stand next to him.

'I don't believe I thanked you for taking care of Nina, did I?' he said.

Shefali shook her head. Her body seemed to be doing things on its own, and she found herself leaning closer to him, tipping her head back and puckering her lips invitingly, leaving him in no doubt about how exactly she wanted to be thanked.

Neil bent his head and, not being able to wait any more, Shefali went up on her toes, dragging his head down with both hands and claiming his lips hungrily with her own. The kiss was explosive, their enforced four-day separation making them desperate. The world seemed to tilt just a little bit for Shefali, and she clung

on to Neil's broad shoulders as she gave herself up completely to the sensation of his hot, eager lips on hers.

'Daddy, should I wear the blue dress or the pink?'
Nina called out from her room.

Neil broke the kiss for a second to say, 'Blue,' before
he slammed the door shut behind him and pulled Shefali back into his arms. This time, however, he buried
his face in the nape of her neck, taking deep shudder-
ing breaths and soothing her trembling body with his
hands before he said huskily, 'Another two seconds and
I wouldn't have been able to stop myself.'

Too shaken to speak, Shefali just nodded, knotting
her fingers in the material of his shirt. He was right to
stop. Her mind acknowledged that. But her body was
clamouring for more. It wasn't fair, being so close to
him and not being able to do more than run her hands
over his fully clothed body. So frustrated that she
could scream, she dug her nails into his arms, feeling the smooth brown skin break under the pressure.
He flinched, but didn't say anything, bending down to
drop butterfly-light kisses on her eyelids.

'Tonight,' he said, and Shefali raised her eyes to his
at the promise in his voice.

'How?' she asked softly, having finally regained control over her vocal cords. 'You can't leave Nina.'

He shook his head vigorously. 'You stay,' he said.
'Have dinner here. Bela's on sedatives, she'll go to bed
early, and the nurse will be in her room. Nina sleeps in
her own room. All we need to do is wait for all of them
to go to sleep.'

He knew he was being reckless, going against all
the rules he'd set for himself, but the feel of Shefali's
body against his was sending a kind of madness cours-

ing through his veins. He could wait till tonight—just about—but not any longer.

Nina was banging on the door, demanding to be let in, and Neil released Shefali to open it. The little girl had changed into her blue frock and was ready to leave. Luckily Neil seemed to have his wits around him, and he managed to get them to the nearest mall without any trouble. Shefali was still so disorientated that she didn't think she was capable of walking in a straight line, let alone driving. She'd regained use of her wits by the time they were in the mall, however, and helped Nina pick out a party dress and a tiny bright-green *salwar kameez* set.

'Let's get you something as well,' Neil suggested to Shefali. 'You can help us celebrate Pujo.'

Nina bounced up and down in excitement. 'Teacher, I saw a *salwar kameez* just like mine in the grown-ups' section. Can you buy it? *Pleeease?* We'll be matching, then!'

Shefali barely suppressed a shudder. Parrot-green looked cute on a four-year-old, but on a full-grown woman it would be hideous. But Nina had grabbed her by the hand and was dragging her towards the shelf where the *salwar kameez* was. Shefali looked back mock-pleadingly at Neil.

'Nina, let Shefali buy what she wants,' Neil said, frowning slightly.

Nina's face fell. 'But we should *match*!' she said, looking up into Shefali's face.

'No,' Neil said brusquely. 'Come on, Nina, let's go and choose a sari for Bela Mashi and let Shefali get on with selecting something.'

He knew he looked far more irritated than the occasion warranted. Unbidden, he was remembering the little bead necklace Nina had given Reema on her last visit to Mumbai. Reema had laughed, and thanked Nina prettily, but she hadn't worn the necklace, and after she'd left he'd found it lying on the sofa where she'd been sitting. The half-possessive, half-imploring look on Nina's little face now was exactly the same as the one she'd worn when she'd spoken to Reema, and it made Neil tense as if in response to a hidden threat.

'Come on, Nina,' he said again.

Nina stood her ground, however, and Shefali intervened quickly before Neil lost his temper. 'Nina, I'll buy the *kameez*, and a white *churidaar* and *dupatta*—what do you think? We'll still match, but I won't be fully in green, so no one will think I'm a tree.'

'Will they think *I'm* a tree, then?' Nina asked, evidently worried.

'Maybe a little plant,' Shefali said. 'Or a big parrot.'

'Or a tall frog,' Nina said, wrinkling her tiny nose.

'Or a green fairy,' Shefali offered.

Nina brightened up. 'Can I have green fairy wings?'

'We can make some,' Shefali promised, giving Neil a quick look. He looked more relaxed now—less as if he was about to swoop down on them and carry Nina away.

'You're good with kids,' he said in an undertone as Nina veered off towards the toy section.

Shefali shrugged. 'I've worked with kids for years,' she said, partly pleased by the compliment, but partly annoyed at the tone of surprise in his voice. In spite of the days she'd spent looking after Nina, he still seemed to think that Nina needed protecting from her.

'Don't we need to get some stuff for you as well?' she asked as Neil collected Nina and the shopping trolley and moved towards the checkout counter. Neil grabbed two XXL *kurtas* from a stack without breaking stride.

'Shopping done,' he announced, and she had to laugh.

'You obviously haven't turned into a self-obsessed TV star yet,' she teased. 'Aren't you going to even try those on?'

Neil dumped the clothes onto the counter. 'Nope,' he said, handing his credit card to the sales clerk. 'If they don't fit I'll give them away.'

'If they don't fit Bela Mashi's going to send you all the way back to pick up more clothes,' Shefali warned. 'Isn't it the eighth day of the festival tomorrow? She said everyone needs to be in new clothes for that.'

'You have a point,' Neil said, and took one of the *kurtas* from the counter. 'Here—hold it up against me and see if it fits.'

Shefali took the long-sleeved tunic and brought it up to his shoulders. In an instant the atmosphere between them changed, as if they were back in his house with the door shutting out the rest of the world. A faint whiff of his aftershave teased at her nostrils, and she had to physically restrain herself from pressing closer to his hard torso. Fully aware of the effect he was having on her, Neil stood absolutely still, and Shefali slid her hands slowly over his chest as she smoothed the *kurta* against his shoulders.

'It fits,' Nina said impatiently, breaking the spell between them with all the subtlety of a sledgehammer. 'Can we pay and go now? I'm hungry, and it's almost night.'

Feeling pretty much the way she had last week, when she'd accidentally switched TV channels from a steamy chick-flick to a Disney cartoon, Shefali hastily put the shirt down.

'Almost done—let's go,' she reassured Nina, jump-ing several inches into the air when Neil's arm snaked around her waist, giving her a very suggestive little squeeze.

'Yes, let's,' he said huskily into her ear. 'I'm looking forward to tonight too…'

Shefali could barely swallow her dinner. They were alone at the table, Nina having eaten early and gone to bed. Bela and her nurse were eating in Bela's room, but they were within earshot, so Neil kept the conversation very neutral, talking mainly about Nina and how she was doing in school.

When they finally got up to put the plates away Neil jerked his head towards his room, and said in an un-dertone, 'Go in there and shut the door. I'll join you in a few minutes.'

Shefali went, her knees suddenly feeling wobbly. She was quite as eager to stay the night with Neil as he was, but the thought of being in the same house as an unaware Nina and Bela was strangely unnerving. For a few seconds she wondered whether she should be sensible and tell Neil that she wanted to go home. But when he strode into the room one look into his smoky blue eyes sent every sensible thought she'd ever had clean out of her head.

'You're beautiful,' Neil said softly.

Shefali trembled as he ran a finger softly down the side of her face and into the neckline of her *kameez*.

'So are you,' she said inanely, but she meant it.

He'd switched off the main light, and the only light

in the room came from a small reading lamp. In its soft golden glow the planes and angles of his perfectly chiselled face reminded her of a painting she'd seen many, many years ago. And his body…

She gasped as his mouth came down on hers, retaining just enough sanity to reach back and switch off the lamp. And then the room was dark, and all she could feel was his lips on hers, and his hands on her body, and she closed her eyes and let the tide of sensation sweep her away.

CHAPTER EIGHT

A SLIGHT SOUND awakened Shefali, and she shifted in bed, making Neil mutter in his sleep and draw her closer. There was a lot of light in the room, though the curtains were closed, and in spite of the quilt she had pulled over herself she was feeling cold. There was a distinct draught coming from the direction of the door, and Shefali looked across to check if it was open.

Nina was standing in the doorway, her doll in her hand, staring at them with wide open eyes.

'Oh, hell!' Neil said, sitting up and pushing his hair off his forehead. 'Nina—come here, sweetheart.'

The little girl stayed poised at the door for a few seconds, then she turned and fled. Muttering a curse, Neil swung his legs off the bed, pulling on his discarded jeans over his boxers.

'T-shirt,' Shefali said, and handed it to him.

He almost snatched it from her, saying in a furious undertone, 'How did the damn door get unlatched?'

Shefali flushed. She had got up in the night to put on her *salwar kameez* and gone out of the room to use the bathroom. Half-asleep, she must have forgotten to latch the door when she came back in.

'I'm sorry—' she said, but Neil was already halfway out of the room, searching for his daughter.

Nina was sitting on the edge of Bela Mashi's bed, clutching her doll to her chest. Neil stopped at the door, his eyes taking in the scene. In the few seconds it had taken him to get dressed Nina had clearly told Bela Mashi pretty much everything she'd seen.

'Are you marrying teacher?' Nina asked, and Bela raised an eyebrow at Neil.

He shook his head. 'Baby, it isn't that simple—' he said.

But Nina cut in. 'You were sleeping in the same bed!' she said. 'Only mummies and papas do that! Is she going to be my new mum?'

'You already have a mum,' Bela said soothingly.

But Nina was on a roll. 'My mum's not here!' she said. 'She di-divorced Dad. So I'm not her kid any more, am I?'

Wishing she could get her hands on Reema's slender, spoilt neck, Bela swept Nina into a hug. 'You're *my* kid,' she said. 'And you're your Dad's kid, and Grandma's kid, and Grandad's and Aunt Anita's, and we all love you—'

'I'm not planning to get married,' Neil broke in, desperate to reassure Nina. Bela gave him a glare.

'But *why* not?' Nina wailed suddenly, taking even Bela by surprise. 'I *want* a mum. Everyone has a mum. And I *like* Shefali Teacher. She's much, much nicer than mum. She talks to Dora and she lets me help roll out the chapattis.'

Neil was about to say that he would let her help roll out chapattis too when Bela intervened.

'Calm down,' Bela said firmly to Nina, but the words

were addressed quite as much to Neil. 'Nina, don't talk about this to anyone. Your dad and Shefali need to sort things out first.'

'I want a mum,' Nina said stonily.

Neil's face twisted in pain. Getting to his feet, he said, 'Not a good enough dad, am I?'

'You're a very worked up dad right now,' Bela said severely. 'I'll look after Nina. For heaven's sake go back to that poor girl you've left alone in your room. I'll speak to the nurse—try and make sure she doesn't talk about this. I'll probably be wasting my breath—I've never met a bigger gossip in my life.'

Neil nodded. The damage he was likely to have done to Shefali's reputation hadn't escaped him, and once again he wished he hadn't given in to the heat of the moment. Letting the lower half of his body take decisions was always a bad idea. He'd already been torn between wanting to make a clean break when he left the city and trying to make some kind of a long-distance relationship work. In a way Bela's broken ankle had come as a relief when it had let him postpone the decision. Now it looked as if he'd made things even more complicated than they already were.

Shefali looked at him warily as he re-entered the room, shutting the door behind him. 'Is she OK?' she asked.

Neil nodded, sitting down heavily on the bed next to her. 'Oh, she's fine,' he said bitterly. 'It's just that she's decided I'm not doing a good enough job as a single father—she wants me to marry you so that she can have a mum.'

Shefali's heart jolted uncomfortably in her chest. The way Neil said it, it sounded as if he thought it was a terrible idea. But for a few seconds she couldn't stop the images floating through her head—her and Neil and Nina—a proper family. She'd always wanted kids, and one of the reasons she'd agreed to marry Pranav was that he'd pretended to be keen on the idea. The thought of Nina wanting her to be her mother was incredibly touching. She'd grown to love the little girl in the few days that they'd spent together—although she'd tried not to show it, just in case Neil mistook it for a trick to keep him hooked.

'She's only four,' Shefali said. 'She'll forget the idea soon enough.'

Neil shook his head. 'I don't think so,' he said. 'She's growing older, and this thing about "everyone else has a mom" is bound to keep cropping up. I'm amazed at how stupid I've been. All this while I thought she'd hate the thought of a stepmother.'

'She might hate it in practice,' Shefali pointed out. 'Right now she only sees the fun side of having a mum. Once she actually has one living in the house with her, telling her to eat her peas and brush her teeth, she might change her mind.'

'Right…' Neil said, and it was evident that even if he'd heard what she was saying he hadn't processed a word of it.

He was clenching and unclenching his fists, and when Shefali put a soothing hand over his he turned quickly to her, gripping her hand in both of his.

'*Have* I done a bad job with her?' he asked, and the vulnerability in his eyes broke Shefali's heart. 'You work with so many children—does it seem like there's something lacking in her life?'

'She's a very well-balanced child,' Shefali said,

choosing her words to make them sound as dispassion-
ate and professional as possible. 'Her vocabulary is advanced for her age, she interacts well with other kids,
and she's emotionally stable.'

And I sound like Maria Montessori, come back from
the dead, Shefali thought to herself.

Seeing that Neil was only partially convinced, she
dropped the teacher act. 'Neil, she's perfectly OK!' she
said. 'Single parents aren't too common in India yet,
so she's bound to ask questions, but that doesn't mean
you pop out of the house and ask the first woman you
see to marry you!'

Which was what he'd almost done, Neil realised. Not
gone out and grabbed the first woman he'd seen, exactly. But he *had* been terribly tempted to ask Shefali
to marry him stopped only by the caution he'd learnt
ever since Nina had become a part of his life.

He sighed. 'You're right,' he said. 'Nina'll be fine.'
He hesitated a little before speaking again. 'This is
going to worsen the gossip about the two of us,' he
said finally. 'Bela's nurse knows we spent the night together—it'll be a miracle if she doesn't tell everyone
in town. And Nina might talk as well. I'm out of here
in a few weeks, but it won't be very pleasant for you.
Maybe we should just tell people that we're engaged so
that they don't give you a hard time?'

'Lie to them, you mean?' Shefali asked, the words
coming out sounding a lot harsher than she'd intended.

Neil shrugged. 'It'd be a white lie—it won't hurt
anyone, and it'll save both of us a lot of explanations
and embarrassment.'

Shefali shook her head automatically. 'No, thanks,'
she said. 'I'll deal with the gossip when I have to, but I

don't think inventing an engagement will help. And it'll confuse Nina even more when you go back to Mumbai and she figures out that we aren't really marrying each other.'

'Take some time and think about it before you reject the idea,' Neil said as he got to his feet. 'Small-town gossip can be pretty vicious. Are you coming with us to the Puja?'

Shefali looked a little thrown by the sudden change in topic.

'I guess…' she said cautiously. 'If you want me to.'

'I do,' he said, giving her a quick smile. 'I need to talk to Nina about this whole thing, and it'll help if you're around. I'll give you some time to shower and get ready—wear that parroty thing we got you yesterday.'

'I'll have to,' Shefali said. 'I slept in this set and it's all crumpled.'

Neil frowned. 'I don't remember you wearing anything when—'

Shefali shoved him crossly. 'Shut up,' she said.

His smile broadened, a wicked twinkle in his eyes. 'You've gone bright pink,' he said. 'Would that be bright pink all over, or just…?'

This time Shefali launched herself at him in a surprisingly good flying tackle. Taken completely off guard, Neil found himself flat on his back on the bed, with Shefali on top of him. She straddled his body, pinioning his arms behind his head.

'No clever remarks,' she said, frowning at him.

'No clever remarks,' he agreed.

'And no jokes about last night.'

'Not a single one,' he said, his voice solemn. Then, when she still didn't release him, 'You *do* realise that

I can grab your hands like this,' he said, suiting action to words, 'and twist you around like this, and you're completely at my mercy.'

'Brute,' she said politely.

'You started it.'

'You did, with your horrible one-liners.'

'Well, OK, but *you* started being violent.'

Very conscious of his hard body pressed against hers, and his smoke-blue eyes looking right into hers, she rallied. 'This is an immature discussion.'

'Very,' he said, squeezing her a little closer and doubling her pulse-rate.

'No one would think you're the father of a four-year-old,' she said.

Neil laughed wryly, releasing her and sitting up. 'A four-year-old who might march in any minute, demanding to know what we're doing,' he said, pushing his hand through his hair. 'You're right. Time to start acting like a responsible adult.'

Not sure if she'd upset him, Shefali countered, 'She'd probably insist we marry immediately. Even a pretend engagement won't be enough.'

'It's a tempting thought,' he said, leaning down to give her a hard kiss. 'I'll go and get breakfast. See you in ten minutes.'

Her head in a whirl, Shefali stared at the closed door. Did he mean that the idea of marrying her was tempting? Or was it a remark he'd just thrown out, not bothering about the implications?

She kept thinking about it while she showered and changed. Marrying Neil… She'd not considered the idea seriously till now, because he'd made it very clear all along that a long-term relationship wasn't on the cards.

And she'd thought *she* didn't want anything long-term either—just a short fling to help her get over Pranav. Somewhere along the line that had changed. Being with Neil was no longer just about the sex—she'd started caring far more than she should.

Shefali's hand stopped halfway through combing her hair as the word 'love' popped into her head, and she stared at her reflection in horror, almost as if she expected to see a gargoyle looking back at her. Where had *that* come from? She wasn't in love with Neil. She couldn't be.

Frantically she started ticking off the reasons one by one. It was only a few months since she'd been about to marry another guy. Right. But that didn't mean anything, did it? Pranav hadn't been the love of her life to begin with, and his betrayal had hurt her pride more than anything else. Next, she hardly knew Neil. On the other hand she'd started sleeping with him after knowing him for only two weeks. If anything, that proved that she was in love. *Scratch that thought.* So, OK, the attraction between them was red-hot, and he was fun to be with, and her heart seemed to shrivel up whenever she thought of him going away—but that didn't mean she was in love, surely? She found the way he pulled her leg annoying, and she had come close to hating him when he'd stopped asking her out once they'd slept together. But hate was a strong emotion too, wasn't it?

Feeling very troubled, she put the comb down and went to find Neil. He was in the living room, on his knees, doing up the little hooks and eyes at the back of Nina's *kameez*. Both of them looked up as she entered the room, and identical smiles lit up their faces. Shefali's heart did a sudden little skip of happiness.

'You wore the green kameez!' Nina was saying, as she ran towards Shefali to stand next to her.

'The parrot ladies,' Neil said, standing up. 'Don't blame me if someone offers you birdseed instead of *bhog* at the *pandal*.'

Nina stuck her tongue out at him and he gave her a mock glare. They seemed to be back on their normal easy footing with each other, and Nina wasn't treating Shefali any differently either. Maybe she'd forgotten about the whole thing—at her age it wouldn't be surprising if she had.

'I'll go and shower,' Neil said. 'By the way, Bela Mashi is hell-bent on coming with us. If you can help her get ready, that'd be great.'

Nina waited till Neil had left the room and said, 'I'm not supposed to talk about you staying in Dad's room.' So she'd not forgotten, then. 'And Dad says I can't bother the two of you and ask you if you're getting married.'

'OK,' Shefali said, and the response sounded weak even to her own ears. No wonder Nina was giving her a slightly exasperated look.

'I'd really like it, though,' Nina said after a pause. 'So would Bela Mashi.'

'Like what?' Shefali asked, feeling stupid. She'd been lost in thought, still trying to gauge her own feelings for Neil, and had completely lost the thread of what Nina was saying.

'If you married Dad,' Nina said.

'Nina…' Shefali said helplessly.

Nina shook her head. 'Bela Mashi said you don't have to say anything. I should just tell you.'

Feeling as if *she* was the four-year-old, Shefali nodded obediently. Bela and Nina had obviously decided everything, and they expected Shefali and Neil to sort out the minor problem of their own confused feelings for each other.

'I'll go and help Bela Mashi,' Shefali said, hoping Bela wouldn't be quite as forthright as Nina was. As it turned out, she was in luck. Bela was more worried about organising the contents of her massive handbag and making sure she had enough money for *prasad* and donations to the temples they were visiting.

Getting Bela Mashi and her wheelchair into the car was a mammoth exercise. Finally Neil had to bodily lift her into the back seat of the SUV and strap the folded wheelchair to the roof. He didn't complain once, or tell Bela off for being so adamant about this whole Durga Puja thing.

Shefali thought of all the other men she knew. Not one would have hesitated to tell a paid employee that they were being a nuisance and couldn't come along. But that was the thing. Neil might pay Bela a hefty salary, but he treated her like one of the family. Also, he made sure that Nina did the same. Shefali had discovered that a lot of teachers and other parents actually thought that Bela was Nina's grandmother, not her nanny. One more point in Neil's favour, Shefali thought as she got into the passenger seat next to him. He was a good person. And nowadays how many people could one say that about?

She gave him a quick look. He was wearing one of the two *kurtas* he'd bought the day before, over jeans, and he looked gorgeous. The dark blue set off his tanned skin perfectly and the colour deepened the grey-blue of his eyes. She had seen him almost every day for the last

few weeks, but today it felt as if she was seeing him for
the first time all over again.

'*Bade hot lag rahe ho*,' she said very fast in Hindi.
You're looking really hot. Bela's Hindi was rudimen-
tary, and that was putting it politely, and Nina wasn't
paying attention.

He gave her a quick smile in acknowledgement, the
corners of his mouth quirking up sexily.

'Not so bad yourself,' he said in an undertone, and
the look in his eyes made Shefali's toes curl up in delight.

The Durga Puja *pandal* was noisy, cheerful and jam-
packed with happy, excited families dressed in their
very best clothes. Neil manoeuvred Bela's wheelchair
as close to the huge painted idol of the goddess and her
children as possible. It was rough going as the marquee
and wooden stage that made up the *pandal* had been
put up on one side of an unused football field. But the
look on Bela's face was worth the effort of pushing the
wheelchair over metres and metres of uneven clumps
of grass. She gazed up into the beautiful, proud face
of the mother goddess with such reverence that a lump
came to Shefali's throat.

'She'll be like this for a while,' Neil said, *sotto voce*.
'Do you want to come and grab something to eat? Neither of us has had breakfast.'

Shefali nodded and followed Neil, while Nina stayed
back with Bela to listen to stories about the goddess.
There was a row of food stalls at one end of the field,
and they stopped at one serving hot *puris* with chick-
pea gravy. The stall owner said something to Shefali
in Bengali, and she gave him a blank look. Neil intervened, answering him in rapid Bengali to the man's evi-

dent surprise. They continued to talk for a few minutes while the man fried their *puris* and served them up.

'What was he saying?' Shefali asked, breaking off a piece of *puri* and dipping it into the gravy.

Neil shrugged. 'Usual stuff. Where did I learn Bengali, I don't look Indian, etc, etc.'

'Do you get a lot of that?' Shefali asked.

He nodded. 'From pretty much everyone I meet. Depending on how sophisticated they are, they either start asking questions the minute they see me or they wait and try to weave it into the conversation. I think I prefer the people who ask directly.'

Shefali tried to think what *she'd* done. She'd noticed his unusual looks, of course, but when she'd met him she'd been too caught up in her own troubles to bother about other people's racial make-up. Her thoughts must have shown very clearly on her face, because Neil laughed and reached out to tuck a stray strand of hair behind her ear.

'That's one of the things I liked most about you when I met you,' he said. 'You weren't interested enough to ask nosy questions.'

Shefali flushed. 'I might have asked if I hadn't been obsessing about my debacle of a wedding,' she said, not wanting to take credit for either very high levels of uninterest or for complete lack of curiosity.

'Well, you didn't,' he said. 'And afterwards...I found lots more to like about you anyway.'

Their eyes met and held for a few seconds, and Shefali felt the little dial in her head swing purposefully towards the 'In Love' indicator. After all, what wasn't there about him to love? Gorgeous, sexy, amazing in bed, fun to be with, kind to little children and old women—he was pretty much perfection walking around on two legs. Feeling a sudden surge of feeling swamp her, she looked away quickly. It wouldn't do to let him know how she felt unless she was one hundred percent sure about it herself. And, more importantly, until she knew whether he returned her feelings.

The frenzied sound of a drum reached their ears and Shefali turned towards the sound, glad of the distraction.

'That's an interesting beat,' she said as they discarded their empty paper plates and began walking back to the *pandal*. 'It's a *dhol,* isn't it?'

'A *dhak*,' Nina corrected her as she bounced up to meet them. 'It's a Bengali instrument—right, Dad?'

'Right,' Neil said. 'Is Bela Mashi OK? Why've you left her there?'

'She's talking to Sinjini's mum and grandma,' Nina said.

Shefali gritted her teeth. Sinjini was in the same class as Nina, and her mother was only a few years older than Shefali. Sinjini's father travelled a lot for work, and Debjani was often stuck in the house with her daughter and her battleaxe of a mother-in-law. She'd made a lot of effort to be friendly with Shefali, but Shefali had avoided her, finding her shallow and very gossipy.

Debjani raised her eyebrows as she saw Shefali with Neil.

'So nice to see you, Shefali,' she said, her eyes darting towards Neil and back to Shefali. 'I didn't know you had friends here—but, no, this is Nina's father, isn't it?'

Very tempted to say that Neil was a person, not an 'it', Shefali gave her a neutral smile.

'Hi, Debjani,' she said. 'Good to see you here.'

Debjani was clearly dying to be introduced to Neil—Shefali gave it exactly two seconds before the nosy questions began.

'Oh, I come here every year. It's a big festival for us. I am so surprised to see *you* here—you're Punjabi, aren't you? Though of course you celebrate Durga Puja in the North too, don't you? Except the idols of the goddess have four pairs of arms, not ten.'

'I've no idea,' Shefali said, not wanting to get pulled into a completely pointless 'my goddess has more arms than yours' debate.

'And you're not Bengali either, are you?' Debjani asked, turning to Neil.

'No,' he said, smiling politely, but with a hint of steel in his gaze.

Debjani's mother-in-law called to her just then, and she hurried away, clearly still dying of curiosity.

'Friend of yours?' Neil asked, his eyebrows raised.

'Can't stand her.'

'Hmm, I wonder why? Come on—let's get back to Bela Mashi.'

They passed Debjani and her mother-in-law, who were chattering away in Bengali. In spite of Debjani's complaints about her mother-in-law the two women seemed on very good terms—perhaps fuelled by their common love for gossip.

Shefali had almost reached Bela when she realised that Neil wasn't next to her any more. Turning, she saw him confronting Debjani and her mother-in-law. His expression was thunderous, and from the completely gobsmacked expression on the two women's faces it looked as if he was giving them the talking-to of their lives.

Bela turned around just at that point. 'You're back!'

she said, smiling—until she looked past Shefali and spotted Neil. 'My goodness—what's happening there?'

'I've no idea,' Shefali said faintly, though she could guess. 'Should I go and find out?'

Bela grabbed her hand in a surprisingly firm grip. 'Don't,' she advised. 'Neil loses his temper very rarely, but when he's like this it's better to stay out of his way. Don't worry,' she said, laughing at Shefali's expression. 'He'll cool down pretty fast. But those women must have done something really nasty for him to lose it like that.'

Neil had turned his back on a very weepy looking Debjani and was striding towards them.

'What happened?' Bela demanded.

'I heard those two *ladies*, say something about Shefali. They didn't bother to lower their voices because they thought neither of us would understand,' Neil said, his voice low and very fierce.

'You told them you're not Bengali,' Shefali said, torn between shock and amusement. She'd never seen this side of Neil before, but it added to his charm, if anything. And the thought that he'd been made so angry by something Debjani had said about *her* felt almost more like a compliment than anything he'd ever said directly to her.

'What did they say?' Bela Mashi demanded, looking almost as annoyed as Neil. She'd developed quite a soft spot for Shefali over the last few days.

Neil shook his head. 'Just common nastiness. You don't need to know.' He swung a chair around and sat down, looking up at Shefali. 'But Shefali does need to know what I said in return.'

Shefali sat down opposite him. The *dhak* was taking

a break, and they no longer had to shout to be heard. She looked at Neil curiously and he took a deep breath.

'Well, here goes. What they were saying wasn't wrong, as far as facts go, it was just the way they said it.' His face clouded over for an instant, and then he shook his head as if to clear it. 'And I was really, really angry...'

'We noticed,' Shefali and Bela interjected simultaneously.

'Yes—so I told them that we're engaged,' he said.

'Engaged!' Shefali said, and her expression was so horrified that something died inside Neil.

After their discussion that morning he'd thought of several more reasons to justify a mock engagement—even a real one—but he hadn't expected Shefali to be quite so upset.

Shefali had found her voice again, and she bubbled into speech. 'But, Neil, that's just... You'll have to go back and tell them it isn't true.'

'No chance,' he said tersely.

'I'll go and speak to them, then,' Shefali said, and she turned and started hurrying across the *pandal*.

She'd hardly gone five metres when Neil caught up with her, grabbing her arm and turning her to face him.

'What's the issue?' he asked.

His voice was so harsh that Shefali flinched back. 'We're *not* engaged,' she wailed. 'And I told you that I didn't want to lie about it. News travels so fast—someone's bound to tell everyone I know in Delhi, and then when we don't get married they'll just think I've been dumped *again*! It'll be a world record—getting jilted twice within two months. I can ask around—there might be someone who's willing to jilt me *next* month, and I'll have a complete hat-trick to boast about in my old age.'

A huge weight lifted off Neil's shoulders and he put his hand against Shefali's mouth to stem the tide of words.

'We don't need to split up immediately,' he said. Then he paused and took a deep breath, voicing the thought that had been clamouring to be heard all morning. 'We don't need to split up at all, for that matter.'

That got her to stop and think.

'Not split up at all?' she said slowly. 'You mean go through with it? Actually get married?'

'It's an idea,' he said. 'Of course if you don't like it we can just stay engaged for some time, and then *you* can do the jilting. As publicly as you like.'

He looked very serious, and Shefali had an absurd urge to giggle. 'We need to talk properly,' she said finally. 'We can't stand here in the middle of a couple of hundred people and sort this out.'

The *dhak* started up again, as if on cue, and Neil shrugged in exasperation, going back to Bela Mashi and saying something in her ear. Bela nodded, and he turned her wheelchair around to move towards the exit.

'Are we leaving already?' Nina asked, sounding disappointed. 'I haven't even had anything to eat.'

'Here—you can eat a piece of *sandesh*,' Bela said, taking a sweet out of the little leaf-wrapped parcel she was carrying.

Neil frowned. 'Is that OK for her to have? Where'd you get it from?'

'It's *prasad*,' Bela said serenely. 'Anything that's been offered to the goddess is pure.'

Nina had already taken the sweet and popped it

into her mouth, and Neil didn't argue further. They'd reached the car, and he repeated his earlier manoeuvre with Bela and the wheelchair, lifting Nina into the back seat with Bela before folding up the wheelchair and getting it onto the roof.

'We'll talk once we're home,' he promised Shefali.

The talk didn't happen, however. They were halfway home when Nina started to complain that she was feeling sick.

'Hang on till we get home,' Neil said, sounding harassed.

Shefali took an empty plastic bag out of her purse. 'Here—use this if you can't hold on till we get there.'

Bela smoothed Nina's hair gently—the little girl was looking very wan and woebegone.

Shefali turned around to smile at her. 'Another five minutes,' she said, and Nina nodded. 'Should I put the radio on? Will that help?'

Nina nodded again, and Shefali put it on, tuning into a channel that was playing Nina's favourite Bollywood song.

Neil frowned. 'I hate her listening to this stuff,' he said.

Hmm, the lyrics *were* rather unsuitable, Shefali thought as she listened to the song a little more closely. But the tune was catchy, and if it kept Nina from throwing up in the car before they reached home it would have served its purpose.

Nina was still holding on when the car pulled up in front of the house. Shefali jumped out and went to her door to help her down. 'Can you manage Bela Mashi?' she asked Neil. 'I'll take Nina in.'

'OK,' Neil said, handing her the keys for the house.

Nina was looking distinctly wobbly, so Shefali picked her up and raced to the door. They'd just about made it to the bathroom when Nina threw up, retching miserably all over the bathmat. Shefali held her head and patted her gently till it was over, getting her to brush her teeth and wash her face before carrying her to her room and tucking her up.

'I want Daddy,' Nina said, keeping her eyes averted from Shefali's. She was feeling desperately embarrassed about being sick in front of Shefali, and her head was beginning to hurt as well.

'He'll be here in a minute,' Shefali said. 'Should I get you some water?'

Nina nodded. Shefali gave her the water and then, seeing that she wanted to be left alone, went into the bathroom to tidy up. Neil found her there ten minutes later.

'For God's sake!' he exploded, leaning in and trying to take the bathmat she was scrubbing away from her. 'What do you think you're doing?

'Cleaning up,' she said, taking the bathmat back and giving it a final rinse before hanging it up in the shower area to dry.

'The maid would have done that!'

'She's taken the day off, remember?'

'Right,' Neil said, and ran a hand through his hair. He looked tired and harried. 'Look, we still need to talk, but—'

'Dad-dee,' came the plaintive call.

'It's OK—go to her,' Shefali said. 'I'll go home now—unless you need any help around here? We can talk later.'

'The nurse should be here in a bit,' Neil said.

'Shefali *didi*,' Bela called from the other room. 'Can you come here for a minute? I need help getting to the bathroom.'

'Coming,' Shefali called back.

Neil looked positively murderous. '*I'll* go,' he said.

Shefali shoved him down in his chair. 'Nina wants you here,' she said. 'And Bela Mashi will probably feel less awkward if I help her.'

Neil buried his head in his hands as Shefali left the room. She was the kind of girl a man would pull out all the stops for on a date—*cordon bleu* meals, refined conversation, music, dancing, expensive gifts, the works. In comparison, he'd treated her to *cholle-puri* on a paper plate, made her the object of vile comments from a pair of nasty-minded women, had her looking after his puking daughter and then mopping the floor afterwards.

And now he was topping it off by relaxing in a chair while she helped his former nanny to the bathroom. Oh, and he'd told the aforesaid pair of nasty-minded women that Shefali was engaged to him. *Way to go, Neil Mitra.* He wouldn't be surprised if Shefali walked out of his house and caught the first flight back to Delhi, just to get away from him.

Nina moaned slightly and grabbed Neil's hand. He turned his attention to her. He suspected that he'd have a lot of time in which to contemplate his own stupidity, but right now his daughter needed him. He smoothed the child's hair off her forehead, wondering if he should call a doctor right away or wait. Wait, probably—she was already looking better, and her eyes were closing as she drifted off to sleep.

He kept on patting her as his thoughts went back to Shefali. The madness that had possessed him ever since

Nina's outburst that morning seemed to have worn off. He had nothing to offer Shefali, he thought bleakly. Other than their being good in bed together, there was no reason she should shackle herself to a man who was expecting her to look after his child, put up with his erratic work schedules and adjust to his frankly over-whelming family. She deserved someone who could give her the kind of glamorous, cosseted life she was used to. Even one of the men her parents had lined up for her would be more suitable than he was.

Shefali popped her head around the door. 'Oh, good, she's sleeping,' she said in a whisper. 'I'll head off home, then, shall I? We can talk when things have quietened down a little.'

'I'll call you,' Neil said, and she nodded, coming across the room to give him a quick hug. Instinctively, his arms came around her and he pulled her closer. *Damn*, it was difficult to think straight with her warm body against his. Memories of the previous night crowded into his head, and his body was eagerly asking for a repeat performance. But it would just have to wait—sex wasn't on the agenda right now.

Hoping it wasn't too obvious quite how aroused he was, he gently released her.

'Talk to you soon,' she said, and gave him a final smile before kissing Nina gently on the forehead and leaving the room.

After she'd gone, Neil realised that he hadn't even thanked her.

CHAPTER NINE

'I DON'T WANT to come home,' Shefali said flatly.

'*Beta*, I know you think we've failed you—' her father began, but Shefali cut in.

'No, you don't get it. I've failed *myself*. I didn't have the sense to stand up for myself when I should have, and I can't blame you for that.'

Her father had been the one to buckle under the strain of Shefali's long absence. After several arguments with her mother he'd called Shefali's Jabalpur number, expecting her to be as happy to hear from him as he was to finally be back in touch with his favourite child. Things hadn't gone to plan, and he sounded almost tearful when he spoke again.

'Look, come back to us. If a career is what you want, the opportunities in Delhi are so much wider— you could do so many things. We thought your getting married quickly after this whole thing with Pranav would be the best solution, but we were wrong. Take your time. There's no pressure—'

'Dad, I've met someone,' Shefali cut in.

There was a stunned silence at the other end of the line as her parents absorbed that piece of information.

'But who?' her mother asked finally, sounding bewildered. 'You said no to Amit, and there wasn't… Oh, my God—you haven't gone and got mixed up with some villager out there, have you?'

'Something like that,' Shefali said, smiling in spite of herself. Anyone from outside Delhi was a villager, according to her mother, with the possible exception of Bombayites.

'Shefali, who is he?' her mother demanded. 'This could be dangerous! You're all alone there—he could be anyone! He could be after your money, or he might just play around with you for a while and dump you. Haven't we had enough scandal over your marriage already?'

'Nothing to do with the marriage was Shefali's fault,' her father intervened. 'But I must admit I'm worried about this, *beta*. At least if we know who he is—'

'You don't need to worry,' Shefali cut in. Her mother's remarks had hurt, though she was doing her best to ignore them. 'I haven't decided anything. And, Dad, don't try coming down here or anything. I'll let you know who he is when I'm good and ready.' Feeling sorry for her father, she added, 'But we can talk about other things as much as you like—about work or the weather or politics. Just not about men and marriage.'

Her doorbell rang and she looked out of the window. Neil was standing on the doorstep, looking rather grim and serious.

'Dad, I need to go,' she said quickly. 'Love you— I'll talk to you later.' She disconnected the call and ran to the door.

'Hi!' she said, hoping she didn't sound as breathless as she felt.

Neil felt his heart twist painfully within his chest. He'd thought long and hard after she'd left, and come to the conclusion that the only thing to do was give She-fali a fair chance to break up with him. He'd have to be careful. She'd been hurt once already, and he'd have to make sure her pride wasn't bruised further.

'Can we talk?' he asked slowly.

'Yes, of course. Come in—don't stand there on the doorstep. Is Nina feeling better now?'

'She is,' he said. 'She's sitting up and taking notice, and she's been asking for mashed eggs for dinner.'

Shefali laughed. Nina loved soft-boiled eggs, mashed up with a spoon and served with salt and no pepper—she would happily eat peanut butter sandwiches and mashed eggs for every meal if allowed to.

'She definitely sounds better,' she said. 'I'll pop by and say hello to her tomorrow.'

'Yes, of course,' Neil said, wondering how to begin.

'I've been thinking,' he said abruptly. 'You were right. I was way out of line when I told those women that we're engaged.'

Shefali felt her heart thud painfully in her chest. Neil's expression was somber—as if he was thoroughly regretting the afternoon's outburst.

'So does that mean you're going to jilt me?' she asked, trying to keep her voice light and failing miserably. 'After all that talk about us not splitting up after all?'

Neil winced. 'No,' he said. 'I *do* want to marry you, but I realise I've put you in a spot. You might not want to marry me—God knows I'm not the catch of the season.'

'Do I have a choice now that you've gone and told the biggest gossip in town that we're engaged?' Shefali asked, the words coming out sharper than she'd meant them to. 'Three people have called me already to ask me if it's true.'

Not to mention that she'd told her parents she'd met someone. But that hadn't been because of Debjani's gossiping. It was just that after Neil had said that they might make the engagement real, she'd started thinking that way. And she'd wanted her parents to know that she could manage without them—that she'd found someone she could be happy with.

Her feelings towards Neil were more muddled than ever. For the last few hours she'd been convinced that she was in love with him. Now she felt like killing him. But the love was still there, turning bitter and beginning to hurt in a way that nothing had hurt her before.

'We'll work that out,' Neil said quietly. 'Like I said, if you don't want to go through with it we can make it look like *you* were the one who changed your mind.'

'I'm not going to lie about it,' Shefali replied. Her voice was firm, but she was a miserable mess inside, convinced that Neil was trying to wriggle out of their engagement. Pride made her go on. 'If I have to, I'll call Debjani and tell her the truth—you were angry and you said the first thing that came into your head.'

Neil bit his lip. He wasn't sure what he'd expected—reassurance, perhaps, that Shefali did actually want to go through with the wedding? It wasn't forthcoming. She looked distinctly upset, but that seemed to be more about the potential embarrassment of a second broken engagement than the thought of not marrying him.

'So what do you want to do?' he asked finally. He was damned if he was going to let her know how much this mattered, but it was a struggle keeping his expression impassive.

'I don't know!' Shefali said, her real feelings breaking through for a moment. 'I'm confused! I need more time to think!'

'Let's leave things as they are for the time being, then,' he said, rallying at the thought of a temporary reprieve. 'Take your time—we don't owe anyone an explanation.'

'Or we can tell them the truth,' Shefali said flatly. 'That we *were* seeing each other but it wasn't ever meant to be serious.'

'That's completely daft,' Neil said, on the verge of losing his temper. 'We've discussed this. There's no point exposing you to the gossip of a bunch of—' His brow creased with worry. 'You've been through a lot already. I don't want to—'

'It's not important,' Shefali cut in. 'God knows, I should be immune to gossip by now.' She turned away and began fiddling with the curtains at the large window that overlooked the school playground. Her eyes were beginning to fill up slowly, and she desperately wanted to be alone. 'Nina'll be waiting for you,' she said over her shoulder. 'You should get back home.'

'Shefali…' he said, wanting to take her in his arms but holding back all the same. 'We can sort this out,' he tried.

But Shefali had had enough. 'I think you should go,' she said again, and resolutely kept her face turned away until she heard the door shut behind him.

The tears were beginning to roll down her cheeks now, and she leaned her head against the windowframe, silent sobs shaking her body. Neil didn't want to marry her and she didn't blame him—he'd offered out of misplaced chivalry and she'd been a fool to take him seriously. She tried to wipe away her tears, but more kept falling, and there was a physical pain in the region of her heart. The intensity of her own reaction scared her. She seemed to have no control either over her tears or over the feeling of utter devastation that had swept over her at Neil's words. She didn't even have the energy to feel angry with herself, or to drag herself away from the curtain and back to her bedroom.

It would probably have made her feel better to know that Neil wasn't in much better shape. Shefali's reaction had confused him—she'd clearly been upset, only he wasn't sure if that was because of the ridiculous situation he'd got her into or because she'd been hurt by his clumsy attempt to give her a way out of it.

He replayed their conversation in his mind. She'd been happy to see him, so she couldn't have been that upset by their 'engagement'—she'd only got agitated when he'd said that pretending to be engaged was a mistake, and the confidence he'd felt in his decision had begun to ebb very rapidly. Shefali had clearly been upset—far more upset than when he'd been out of line, mouthing off to Debjani. So maybe… A ridiculous little tendril of hope started unfurling in the region of his heart.

He was at the end of the lane the school was in, and he turned back to look up at Shefali's flat. It was nearing dusk, and he could see her slim figure silhouetted against the curtain in exactly the same position that he'd left her in. There was an appearance of utter defeat in her stance, and Neil suddenly couldn't take it any more.

Shefali jerked away from the window in shock when he came up the stairs two at a time and pushed open the door. Her cheeks were still tear-stained, and her hands instinctively went up to cover her face. The vulnerability of the gesture stripped the last of Neil's doubts away, and he crossed the room in two quick strides to take her in his arms.

'Don't,' he said, as she made to push him away. 'I'm sorry. I'm *so* sorry.'

He took her into his arms and this time she didn't resist. For the moment she felt too broken to be anything other than grateful for the strong arms around her. She felt completely drained, but the tears weren't stopping, and they were washing away the confidence she'd carefully built up over the last two months.

Neil didn't say anything, just held her close and stroked her hair till her sobs finally faded into silence. Even then he kept holding her, handing her a tissue to dry her face and then pulling her closer and pressing his lips to her hair.

'I'm sorry,' he said once again, and Shefali finally pulled back to look into his face.

'Why did you come back?' she asked quietly.

The embarrassment of having spent a good fifteen minutes crying into his chest was beginning to hit her. If he was here just to make himself feel better about ditching her she'd made an utter fool of herself. She began to feel the stirrings of anger within her—both at herself for making her feelings so apparent and at Neil for rejecting a chance of happiness together.

'Well?' she prompted when Neil didn't reply.

Neil pushed a hand through his thick hair. 'I don't know,' he admitted honestly. 'I just couldn't bring myself to walk away. I guess I don't really know what I want for myself, but I *do* want you to be happy.'

'You don't want to be with me,' Shefali said flatly. 'I

think you made that quite clear. You can't force your-self to feel differently, and I don't blame you for that. Instead of feeling sorry for me you should just put the whole thing out of your head. You're only complicat-ing things for both of us.'

'I do want to be with you!' he said, so forcefully that Shefali looked up in surprise. 'I thought it'd be best for you if I stayed away, but you evidently don't feel the same.' He allowed himself a brief smile. 'Oh, and by the way, if I'm feeling sorry for anyone it's myself, so you can get off your high horse.'

In spite of the mixed emotions raging through her, Shefali couldn't help laughing a little at the last sen-tence. He was right—that *was* what rankled the most: the thought that he might be pitying her.

'So that's OK, then,' she said, this time actually man-aging to keep her voice steady and her tone light. *Well done, Shefali*, she said to herself. *Maybe a career on the stage is within reach after all.* 'If you're not feeling sorry for me, you're forgiven. But I don't get it—*why* do you think it'd be better for me if you stayed away? You were worried about Nina earlier, but she seems fine with it, so...'

'I'm not ideal husband material,' he said. 'I've been married once before, I have a kid, and I'm not even sure how I really feel about you—it's a complete rec-ipe for disaster.'

'I'm not sure how I feel about *you* either,' Shefali said. 'Sometimes I hate you. But then sometimes I think we could make it work. If both of us tried hard enough.'

She looked up at Neil, and her expression was such a mixture of determination and vulnerability that he bent down and kissed her. The kiss lasted a lot longer than he'd planned. Shefali's soft lips were an unbearable temptation against his own. It took his last ounce of self-control to pull away.

'You'd be taking on a lot,' he said warningly. 'You saw what this morning was like—and that's just with Bela and Nina around. You haven't even met the rest of the family.'

'And *you* haven't met mine,' Shefali countered. 'Ten minutes with my mother and you'll be wondering why you agreed to come within five feet of me.' She hadn't missed the look in his eyes, and little tendrils of hope were beginning to spring up. Perhaps he *did* care for her after all, and only some quixotic scruples were holding him back from saying it.

'So we stay engaged, then?' Neil said after a brief pause, and broke into his boyish, slightly lopsided and utterly charming smile. 'Let's go buy you a ring.'

That smile had helped triple the ratings of his shows, and Shefali was far from being immune to it. For a few seconds she was too busy trying to control her heart-rate to grasp fully what he'd said.

Then, when he took her hand and started pulling her towards the door, it sank in, and she yelped, 'What? Right now?'

'Why not?' he said. Neil had always had a slightly reckless streak in him—he'd suppressed it ruthlessly for the last few years, but it was back with a vengeance now.

Shefali balked, however. 'Maybe you should take a day or two to think it over,' she said. 'I feel like I'm rushing you into this.'

'You're not,' he said, bending down and giving her a swift, hard kiss that robbed her of all power to object. 'I'm the one who's in charge of the rushing. Now, come on—let's go get you that ring. What would you like? Diamonds? Emeralds? Sapphires?'

Shefali was already shaking her head. 'Not diamonds,' she said, thinking of the ring Pranav had got her—the one she'd sold before leaving Delhi.

'I'm not too fond of them either,' Neil said, and they looked at each other and laughed.

'Let me guess—you got Reema a solitaire?' Shefali said.

'Marquise cut, with smaller diamonds by the side,' he said. 'Reema left it with me for Nina when she grows up.'

A shadow crossed his face, and for a second Shefali wondered if he was having second thoughts. Then his expression cleared and he took her hand.

'No diamonds, then. Let's get to the store and see what they have.'

It took them almost two hours, and trips to four jewelers, before they found a ring Shefali liked. It was in white-gold filigree, with no gemstones, and she fell in love with the intricate design as soon as she saw it.

'That one,' she said.

The shop assistant gave Neil a quick look. Pretty much everyone in town knew Neil by sight because of the TV show and the frenzy in the local press around it.

'It's a nice ring, sir, but it's not really for daily wear. It'll be difficult to clean, and…'

'And evidently you don't think it's suitable for an engagement ring?' Neil cut in, sounding amused. 'This is the one she likes, so we'll take it.'

'Can I put it on now?' Shefali asked as they left the store. 'Or do we need to tell our families officially first?'

'I was thinking of a small engagement party,' Neil said. 'Maybe next week? That will give everyone time to get used to the idea.'

Shefali's eyes widened. 'Wow—you don't waste time, do you? Three hours ago you wanted us to split up. Now you're planning engagement parties. Next you'll be talking to wedding caterers and quarrelling about the decorations on the cake.' In a way, his wanting to get engaged in a hurry was flattering, but she couldn't help wondering if he wanted to make things official before he had a chance to change his mind again.

Neil stopped in the middle of the pavement and swung Shefali around to face him. 'Look at me,' he said, and when Shefali laughed he said, 'No, I'm serious. Look at me.'

She looked into his eyes, and her laughter stilled under the intensity of his gaze.

'I care about you,' he said. 'I have since the day I first kissed you. But it took me a long time to come to terms with it. I've got so used to putting Nina first that I assumed I wouldn't be able to have a serious relationship with anyone until she was a lot older.' He paused, and then said, 'I tried to keep telling myself that what you and I shared was just friendship and good sex, but it's so much more than that.'

He touched her cheek, and the light touch sent Shefali's body up in flames.

'Trying to walk away from you was the hardest thing I've ever done in my life. I didn't think I was right for you. I thought the only person I was hurting was myself.'

'Care', not love, Shefali noted, but there was no doubting his sincerity. And *love* was such an over-used

word anyway. Perhaps this was a better foundation for
a relationship than both of them claiming to be madly
in love with each other? Though in her case it would
be a simple statement of fact. She'd finally admitted to
herself that she loved Neil. He didn't return the feeling,
but that was something she could live with as long as
they were together.

Her hand came up to grip his tightly. 'I think we're
right for each other,' she said. There was a lot more that
she wanted to say but it could wait—this was the most
important thing.

'Right, so we'll get engaged at a party next week,
then?' Neil said, taking her hand and resuming their
walk towards the car. He gave her a mischievous look.
'Unless you want some time to think it over?'

Shefali shook her head. Her parents would want
her to get engaged in Delhi, but she couldn't stand the
thought of the same crowd of friends and relatives who'd
been at her first engagement party standing around and
gossiping at this one.

'Next week is fine,' she said. 'I'll tell my parents.
Will yours be coming down?'

'I'll have to tell them first,' he said. 'I'm sure they'll
come—it's a long trip, and there are no direct flights,
but they'll want to be here. Not so sure about my sister,
though. She's on the tea estate, and it's high up in the
hills—we can patch her in on a video link.' At Shefali's
puzzled look, he said, 'We video conferenced Nina's
last birthday party so that my parents could see her cut
her cake. It works quite well.'

Shefali tried to imagine her own pomp-and-show-
obsessed mother attending her engagement party
through satellite link, failed, and began to laugh.

'Your family's a lot more tech-savvy than mine,' she said. 'Mine will expect to be flown down and met at the airport by a chauffeur-driven car, and they'll turn up their noses at everything they see.'

Neil tried not to look appalled. What little he'd heard of Shefali's parents hadn't endeared them to him.

'You'll have to break it to them gently,' he said as they reached the car and got in. 'Getting engaged to a divorced man who has a child isn't what most parents plan for their daughters.'

'Well, most parents don't get their daughters engaged to men who walk out on the wedding day either,' Shefali retorted, her eyes beginning to flash. 'They're hardly in a position to comment. If they don't like it they needn't come. Actually...' She pulled her phone out of her handbag and began to dial her father's number. 'Let me tell them right now.'

Neil had been about to pull out of the parking lot, but he stopped the car. 'Shefali, are you sure?' he asked, his expression half-amused and half-alarmed. 'You're working yourself into a temper even before you speak to them.'

'That's what works best,' she said, pressing the green 'dial' button on her screen. 'Hi, Dad,' she said, when her father picked up on the first ring. 'You remember what I was telling you earlier? Well, I've decided to get engaged. We're having an engagement party next week, and it'd be lovely if you and Mum could come.' She waited for the expostulations to die down, and went on. 'Yes, of course I'll tell you more about him.'

Neil took the car on to the main road, and began driving towards his bungalow. They needed to tell Nina and Bela Mashi as well, and it would be best to do it together. Judging from Shefali's side of the conversation, she seemed to have things well under control.

'Well, for starters, his name's Neil Mitra,' she said. 'Yes, the guy who comes on TV. Yes…Yes…No, I hadn't seen the show before I met him, Dad. He was here shooting a section of his next show and I ran into him by accident.'

There was a pause, and Neil could hear an agitated female voice join the conversation.

'No, Mum, he's not Punjabi. He's half-Bengali and half-British.'

Pause…

'*British*, mum—his mother's…' She raised an eyebrow at Neil and mouthed, 'English? Scottish? What?'

'English,' he mouthed back.

'English,' Shefali said into the phone. 'Yes, English. His parents met at Oxford.' She paused as her parents shot more questions at her.

'His father has a tea estate, I think,' she said, 'but he's retired now. Neil's sister manages the estate.' She looked at Neil for confirmation and he nodded.

There were some more squawks from the phone.

'I don't know, Mum!' she said exasperatedly. 'Wait, I'll ask him. She wants to know if you're Hindu or Christian,' she said.

'Well, neither,' Neil said, looking a little bewildered. 'I'm not particularly religious.'

'What do you put on government forms and stuff?'

'Hindu.'

'He's Hindu,' Shefali reported into the phone. 'And he lives in Mumbai, so I guess I'll be shifting there too. As soon as I can arrange it with the school.'

The squawks emanating from the phone had lessened

in intensity, so Neil assumed that her parents were OK with the news so far.

'Tell them about Nina,' he said softly, bracing himself for their reaction.

Shefali nodded. 'Dad, Mom—there's one more thing, and it's important, so listen to what I'm saying carefully.' There was a muted sound of assent from the phone. 'Neil has a daughter—no, Mum, *listen* to what I'm saying. He's not married. I wouldn't be getting engaged to him if he was, would I? The laws against bigamy are pretty strict.'

She took a deep breath.

'Nina's one of my students. She's four years old, and she's adorable. Neil and her mother split up years ago, and they're still on good terms.'

There was a long pause as her parents digested that piece of information. Shefali found herself digging her nails into her palm. Perhaps telling her parents when Neil was around had been a bad idea. Lord knew what her mother would come out with now, and if she said something about Nina Shefali knew she wouldn't be able to stop herself from hitting back.

'Shefali, do you love him?' her father asked finally, and the words sounded odd coming from someone who'd always been a very contained and formal person.

'Yes,' she whispered, looking at Neil and knowing that it was true. Caring was all very well, in its place, but what she felt for Neil was something far more elemental.

'Well, that's all that's important,' her father said. 'And we've always wanted a granddaughter, so tell Nina and Neil that we're looking forward to welcoming them to the family.'

'Thanks, Dad,' Shefali said, and she felt tears well into her eyes. All her life she'd felt her father's love was dependent upon her toeing the line and doing what he wanted. She'd misjudged him—it looked as if things were going to turn out well after all.

But she'd temporarily forgotten her mother.

'I suppose it's OK,' her mother was saying. 'He seems to be from a good family, and he's doing well—and after that whole thing of your wedding being cancelled and you leaving Delhi like that I guess a divorcé's not such a bad deal. I've been asking around, and it'll be difficult to marry you off now that you've said no to Amit and people know you've left town. I knew that was a bad idea. Everyone just assumes that *you* were at fault in some way…'

'Mallika, stop running on,' her father said, to Shefali's intense relief. 'If Shefali left home it was because she didn't get the support she needed from her own parents and she thought she'd be better off on her own.'

'I should have known you'd take *her* side,' her mother muttered. 'I've slaved over the children, bringing them up alone while you were travelling all over the country, but of *course* when things go wrong you're on their side. How old is this Neil anyway?' she asked, switching battle fronts abruptly and taking Shefali off guard. 'Must be in his thirties if he's got a four-year-old. That's not so bad—around ten years older than you. Though of course nowadays—'

'He's twenty-eight,' Shefali interrupted before her mother could launch into a thesis on age differences between spouses. 'Look, you can ask him the story of his life when you meet him. The engagement party will be next week, and we want you to be here.'

Long pause.

'No, we don't want to get engaged in Delhi… Yes, his parents are fine with it… Yes, we do have hotels here, Mum. It's not a village. We're planning to have a quiet do at home, with just family and a few friends. You can stay with me—there's lots of space… Yes, Mum… Yes, Mum. I'll tell you as soon as we decide the date…Yes… Thanks, Dad. Love you guys too.'

'That sounded as if it went quite well,' Neil said after she'd rung off. 'From the way you described them I thought they'd be extremely upset.'

'Dad's changed,' Shefali said wonderingly. 'He sounded almost human—either it's old age catching up, or an alien spirit's taken over his body.'

Neil hesitated a little. 'Or maybe he's more shaken up by your leaving home than you think?' he said.

'What do you mean?'

'I was thinking how *I'd* feel if I'd arranged a marriage for Nina and something went wrong and she left home. It would hurt very badly. I'd think I'd failed her, and I'd be willing to do anything to get her back.'

Shefali gave him a weird look.

'Are you channelling the same spirit Dad is? Because that's almost exactly what he said—about failing me and stuff like that.'

Neil shrugged. 'Comes with being a parent,' he said. It was at times like these that he felt immeasurably older than Shefali, despite the fact that there was only a one-year age-gap between them. 'We're home. Let's go and break the news to Nina and Bela Mashi.'

Nina took the news very calmly. As far as she was concerned the arrangement had been a done deal ever since she'd let both parties know what she wanted.

'The entire universe conspires to give you what you want? Is that it?' Bela Mashi asked, misquoting a line from a popular Bollywood movie in her heavily accented Hindi. 'At least congratulate your dad and Shefali Teacher.'

Nina obediently congratulated them, and then trotted off to watch something on TV.

Neil's parents' reaction was far more gratifying, and so was his sister's. Both his mother and sister insisted on speaking to Shefali, and after talking to them for a few minutes Shefali felt as if she'd known them all her life. Barbara Mitra was warm and friendly, and Anita brimmed over with energy.

'Of *course* I'm coming there for the engagement party!' she exclaimed. 'Even if I have to drive all the way.'

'You won't have to,' Neil said, taking the phone from Shefali. 'Though you might have to fly to Nagpur and drive down from there.'

Anita groaned. 'You *had* to hide yourself in a little up-country hole, didn't you?' she said.

'Well, while we're on the subject, you're not exactly in a bustling metropolis either. It's almost impossible to get through to you. I called the cell-phone company for help, and they said it takes a while to convert drumbeats to cell-signals.' Neil put the phone down while his sister was still spluttering at him and grinned.

'All the important people told?' Shefali asked.

'There's only Reema left,' Neil said. 'I need to let her know, but it can wait. I'll e-mail her tomorrow.'

It was on the tip of Shefali's tongue to ask *why* Reema needed to be told when Neil answered her unspoken question.

'It's part of our custody agreement for Nina,' he said. 'We need to inform each other if we shift cities, or re-marry, or change jobs. But I'd have told her in any case. She's been part of my life for so long, even though she's not particularly involved with Nina.'

'Yes, of course,' Shefali said, but she felt a strange emotion—not jealousy, exactly, but a feeling that she'd missed out on so much of Neil's life, when he'd been younger and less careworn. All those years had gone to Reema, and they'd been wasted on her.

Feeling quite fiercely possessive about Neil, she went across the room, and planted a kiss firmly on his lips.

'Hey, Nina and Bela might come in at any moment,' Neil said, gently disentangling himself from her arms.

Shefali shrugged and stepped back a few inches. Gently, she loosened a button on Neil's shirt and put her hand under the crisp cotton, sliding it over his smooth brown skin till her hand was directly over his heart. She could actually feel his heartbeat quicken, and she gave him a triumphant little smile as he groaned under his breath and pulled her into his arms.

CHAPTER TEN

THE ENGAGEMENT PARTY came and went in a flurry of activity. Neil's parents and sister came down to Jabalpur for it, and so did Shefali's parents. Shefali's mother was the only one who didn't seem entirely pleased, and Shefali heaved a sigh of relief after she'd seen her parents off at the airport.

'My mum drives me bananas,' she confided to Neil over a cup of coffee at their favourite café. 'She seems to think that if I'd only gone back to Delhi she'd have got me a maharajah to marry at the very least.'

Neil laughed. 'I can't blame her for thinking I'm not a very good catch,' he said. 'She'll probably resent my existence for the next twenty years.'

'Oh, she'll come around once we have kids,' Shefali said. 'She's nuts about my nephew, and she was trying to hide it but she took quite a fancy to Nina as well.'

Neil hardly heard the last part of the sentence. *Once we have kids.* He felt as if she'd punched him in the stomach. And she'd said it so casually, as if it was a perfectly natural thing—which, to be fair, it was. God, he'd been so stupid and short-sighted, rushing into an engagement without clearly spelling things out to Shefali.

He looked away for a few seconds, and when he

turned back to her his face had a steely expression on it that made Shefali's heart sink all the way down to her stilettos.

'Shefali, I thought you knew,' he said. 'I don't want any more kids.'

Shefali stared at him in dismay.

'You mean…?'

'I mean no more children,' he said heavily. 'I don't think I can go through the experience all over again. At least it's not something I'm ready for right now.'

'And you thought I'd be OK with that?'

'I told you,' he said, though he realised now that it hadn't registered. 'The night we had that argument— before Bela broke her leg.'

'That was *aeons* ago!' Shefali said in disbelief. 'You also said that you'd never remarry—how was I supposed to know you meant part of it and not the whole thing?'

'I realise that,' Neil said. 'And I'm sorry. But I don't want more children. I should have talked to you about it again before—'

'But *I* want kids!' she interrupted, her voice shaking in her agitation. 'I love Nina, but I want to have children of my own as well. Not right away, but in a few years. And you won't be bringing up a child alone this time. It isn't the same thing at all!'

'That's not the only reason,' Neil said. 'It wouldn't be fair to Nina. She's used to being the centre of my life. If we have a child together it would make her feel excluded—as if she's being sidelined out of my life. And there'd be a huge age-gap between her and any child we had. It'd be like a whole new family that she's not a part of.'

Holding on to her temper with difficulty, Shefali

said, 'It would probably do her good, having a sibling. Being an only child isn't very healthy.'

'I think *I'm* the best judge of what's good for my daughter,' Neil said.

At that, Shefali stood up abruptly, pushing her chair back. 'I thought the whole point was that she was going to be my daughter too,' she said quietly.

Neil looked up at her. 'Would you still think of her as your daughter if you had a child of your own?' he asked.

Shefali gave him a long, steady look. 'I can't believe we're having this conversation,' she said. 'And I can't believe you're telling me the day after we get engaged that you don't want to have more children.'

'I thought you already knew,' Neil said. 'I've spent the last four years caring for Nina, and I don't regret it—not for a minute—but now that she's a little older and more independent I don't want to start the whole cycle all over again. It probably seems appallingly selfish to you, but that's the way I feel.'

Shefali sat down again slowly.

'I've always wanted children,' she said. 'There was a huge age gap between me and my older brother, and he left home for college when I was still quite little. It was like being an only child. I always used to think that when I got married I'd have at least three children, so that the house would be full of kids playing and having fun.'

'I can understand that,' Neil said. 'But I can't change the way I feel. If you're uncomfortable with it there's still time—we can postpone the marriage, or even cancel it if that's what you want.'

He said it casually, but his hands were clenched

tight—Shefali, however, was too upset to notice his agitation.

'No, we're not cancelling the wedding,' she said fiercely. 'I can't have another broken engagement. It'd kill my parents. We'll just have to work this out.'

'Assuming we *can* work it out,' he said, 'I would ideally like to avoid a second divorce as well.'

Shefali looked away, but not fast enough, and Neil's expression changed when he saw the deep hurt in her eyes.

'God, I'm sorry,' he said, reaching out and taking her hand even as she tried to pull away. 'No, I mean it. I don't know what's got into me. I'm being a complete jerk.'

Shefali gently disengaged her hands from his. 'Neil, if you want to call the whole thing off tell me honestly,' she said. 'I can handle the mess that comes with it. Don't try and push me into calling it off for you.'

Neil groaned. 'Sweetheart, I don't want to call it off. Let's talk about this properly later. We're both too worked up to be able to discuss it rationally right now.'

Shefali didn't think she'd ever be able to rationally discuss the prospect of never having children of her own, but she nodded, and they finished their coffee in silence.

Neil stared grimly out of the nearest window. He couldn't help thinking that they'd have been better off if he'd resisted temptation and stayed away from Shefali in the first place. Now he couldn't bear the thought of not being with her. Had he walked away two months ago he'd have kept her from getting hurt as well. But as things were right now they seemed headed for certain disaster—the most optimistic bookie wouldn't lay odds in favour of their relationship surviving a year.

'It's ironic,' Shefali said suddenly. 'Reema didn't want to have a child, and you forced her to. I *do* want to have babies, and you're telling me you don't want them.'

Neil tensed immediately, and she wished she'd kept her mouth shut.

'It's not the same thing,' he said.

'I'm not saying it is,' Shefali said, getting to her feet. 'It's something that struck me, that's all. Let's go. I have a set of lesson plans to go through for next week.'

Except that the lesson plans could have been written in Ancient Greek for all the sense she could make of them. Her head was pounding in misery. She'd thought she could handle Neil not being in love with her, but not wanting children was something else altogether. For as long as she could remember she'd wanted babies—she'd even chosen to work in a playschool so that she could spend time with children before she had some of her own.

Her first impulse when Neil had told her he didn't want kids had been to call off the engagement. But the thought of spending the rest of her life without him was too unbearable to contemplate. She'd told him she didn't want to break off the engagement because her parents would be devastated—which was true. Only she was beyond such considerations now. The embarrassment of a broken engagement had seemed important when it was Pranav, but Neil meant so much more to her. She couldn't think of anything other than the fact that she wouldn't be able to live without him.

There was, of course, the possibility that he'd change his mind. Shefali smiled grimly. Betting her own happiness on Neil's unlikely change of heart was so feeble that it was funny.

The phone rang and Shefali picked it up. 'Yes, Neil?' she said, her voice flat, though her heart was thumping so hard she could barely hear herself think.

'I was thinking about what you said,' Neil said quietly. 'About my forcing Reema to have the baby and telling you I don't want kids.'

'OK…' Shefali said, not knowing how to respond. Where was he going with this? Had he changed his mind after all? And if he hadn't, why was he calling her?

'You were right. I'm not being fair to you, and I probably wasn't being fair to Reema either.' Neil paused for a second, not sure how to phrase what he had to say next. He'd thought about the situation from every possible angle, and there was only one solution he'd been able to come up with. 'If we do have a kid, it would be your responsibility,' he said. 'I mean, I'd provide for it financially and everything, but you'd need to be prepared to bring it up on your own.'

'On my own?' Shefali repeated after him like an automaton, anger stirring within her for the first time. 'You mean you wouldn't acknowledge the baby?'

'I would,' he said. 'I do care for you, and I hate the thought of you being unhappy—'

'You just don't hate it enough to bring yourself to have children with me,' Shefali said bitterly. Nothing had changed, and she'd been naïve to assume that it would.

'So, *Nina's* your child, but my son or daughter wouldn't be? Is that it?' Shefali asked. 'Neil, that's so cold-blooded I don't know what to think. If anything, it's worse than not having children at all.'

Neil's hand tightened on the phone. He was finding it impossible to explain to Shefali what he was going through, but it looked as if he wouldn't have to—Shefali sounded so coldly furious that she'd probably break off their engagement in the next sentence.

'It's not about you,' he said quietly. 'It was a thought,' he said. 'Like I said, if it were down to me I wouldn't have more children.'

'If it were down to you, you wouldn't have proposed to me either,' Shefali said, an immense sense of weariness settling on her. It was no good battling this and pretending that she could make it work when Neil was so clearly not interested. 'I'm sorry, Neil. I threw myself at your head and I've put you into this situation. Let's forget the whole thing, shall we? You'll be a lot happier without me, and I'll survive without you.' She took a deep breath. 'Have a good life,' she said, and cut the call, switching her phone off for good measure. 'So that's that,' Shefali said out loud.

To her own surprise, she didn't feel like crying or breaking things—she felt numb, as if someone very close to her had just died. Pulling a shawl around her, she went to stand by the window. This time Neil wasn't likely to come rushing over to make up, but she couldn't help glancing out. Just in case. The only person in sight was the neighbourhood night watchman on his rounds, and she closed the window with a bang and drew the curtains.

She was quite calm as she went around the flat, putting off the lights, but when she got into bed and picked up a book to read her eyes fell on the ring on her engagement finger. A giant hand seemed to squeeze her heart, and she bit her lower lip to suppress the tears that sprang to her eyes. She put her book down on the bedside table, took the ring off, and put it carefully on top of the book. Only then did she let the tears flow, switching off the bedside lamp and burying her face in the pillow so that she couldn't hear the sound of her own sobs.

Nina didn't come to school the next day, and Shefali was glad. She wouldn't have been able to behave normally around her, and she didn't want the bubbly little child being affected by what was essentially a grown-up quarrel.

'Are you feeling all right?' one of the teachers asked curiously as she helped Shefali lock up her office.

'Bit of a headache,' Shefali said briefly. She hadn't told anyone that her engagement was off. She wasn't sure if Neil had told Nina yet, and in any case the thought of talking about it was as appealing as a multiple root-canal.

If she was honest with herself, she knew she hadn't wanted to break up with Neil—the previous night had been absolutely miserable as she'd tossed and turned, replaying everything she and Neil had said to each other in her mind. Only her bruised pride had stopped her from calling him. That and the thought that he might change his mind—*again!*—and come to her. Well, he hadn't. Perhaps he was glad to be rid of her. Or was he expecting her to come crawling back to him on her own?

Shefali's hands curled unconsciously into fists by her sides. The pain in her heart was almost unbearable. She might do it—go to him and beg him to take her back. However much it went against the grain.

'That old lady's waiting for you outside,' one of the school helpers came in to say. 'Nina's nanny.'

'I'll be out in a minute,' Shefali said, and her heart began to race.

She could think of no reason for Bela to be at school—unless she'd come to tell her that they were leaving, that Nina wouldn't be coming back. Hurriedly, she pushed her hair away from her face and retied it with a scrunchie, glancing into a mirror to check that she looked composed enough. In spite of her age, Bela had sharp eyes, and Shefali didn't want her picking up on quite how disturbed she was feeling.

'Good to see you, Bela Mashi,' Shefali said. 'How's the ankle?'

Bela looked up, and smiled, but the smile didn't quite reach her eyes. She looked tired, and old.

Shefali instinctively put a hand out to her. 'Are you OK?' she asked.

'Can I speak to you?' Bela said without answering the question. 'I would have called before coming, but I didn't have your number.'

'Yes, of course,' Shefali said, helping Bela up and taking her into one of the empty classrooms. A couple of the teachers gave her odd looks as she settled Bela onto a chair with a stool for her injured ankle. Shefali went to the door and shut it, then came back to Bela.

'I'm not going to ask you what happened,' Bela said. 'But Neil told me today that he's not sure if you're getting married after all.' She paused a little, then said flatly, 'He's very unhappy.'

Right. Shefali felt hot anger bubble up, but before she could say anything Bela continued.

'He said it's his fault. And he told me not to try talking to you.'

'And so you came here as soon as you could?' Shefali said sarcastically.

Bela gave her a steady look. 'Yes, I did,' she said, and Shefali immediately felt ashamed of herself. 'I'm an old woman, and I don't always do as I'm told.'

'I didn't mean…' Shefali began to say, and Bela waved a hand at her.

'I know you didn't,' she said. 'And I'm not trying to interfere. But I can't see him like this.'

There was a long pause as Bela ineffectually dabbed at her damp eyes with the corner of her sari. She was completely unselfconscious, but Shefali was beginning to feel horribly embarrassed.

'I started working for Barbara *didi* when Neil was born,' Bela said after a while. 'He was such an affectionate child, but very headstrong—didn't listen to anything *didi* or I told him. He'd climb trees and fall out of them, get into fights with the bullies in school, try crazy stunts on his bicycle—we had to patch him up almost every day. He never cried, though, even when he had blood pouring out of a cut. He'd just bite his lip and wait till we'd bandaged it, and then he'd be off again, looking for trouble. He calmed down a lot when he got into his teens—we were surprised. We'd thought he'd get worse, but that was the time he met Reema. They were so busy with school and drama classes and her singing that he didn't have time to get up to mischief. And then, before we knew it, they grew up, and Nina was on her way. Reema didn't want the baby…'

'They were both very young,' Shefali offered when the pause became awkward.

'It's been tough for him,' Bela was saying. 'Bringing up Nina alone, giving up so many things in his career so that he could be with her. He used to be a warm, impulsive boy, but he's changed so much even I can't see the old Neil in him sometimes.'

'I don't know why you're telling me this,' Shefali said, the awkwardness creeping back. 'Especially if Neil doesn't know you're here.'

Bela sighed, and again Shefali thought how old she looked.

'I'm not going to pry and ask what went wrong,' Bela said. 'But Neil needs you. If you can find a way to forgive him for whatever he's done I wanted to ask you to give him another chance.'

'Some differences aren't reconcilable,' Shefali said helplessly. 'He hasn't done anything that needs forgiving.'

'He needs you,' Bela repeated, getting slowly to her feet. 'So does Nina.'

Shefali went back to her flat after ushering Bela out, feeling more confused than she'd ever been before. She sat down at her dining table and tried to have it out with herself. Nothing Bela had said actually changed anything as far as her decision to break off with Neil went, but it had made her think about him differently. And to hope a little.

She reached out for her phone. If nothing else, they needed to talk before they declared the split final. Her phone was still switched off—she'd been too upset in the morning to remember to switch it on. It began to beep as soon as it caught a full cell signal, and last night's text messages started to come in.

There were several from Neil.

Can we talk?

Need to speak to you. I'm sorry I upset you.

I can't get through to you. Call me back whenever you can.

Shefali switched the phone off again. Some things needed to be discussed face to face. It took her twenty minutes to get to Neil's house, and she asked the auto-rickshaw driver to wait for her. 'I don't know how long I'll take,' she said, handing him a fifty-rupee note. 'And I might need to go somewhere else if the person I need to meet isn't at home.'

'Neil Sir's at home,' the rickshaw driver informed her smugly. 'His car's parked in the driveway.'

So it was. And of course the auto-wallah knew all about Neil—he probably even knew they'd had an argument. The joys of small-town life.

Shefali's hand trembled a little as she rang the doorbell. She had no idea what she was going to say to Neil—it was one thing telling herself that she needed to fight for their relationship to survive and quite another actually doing it. For a few seconds she contemplated going back home and calling him after all, but the door opened before she could do more than take a step back.

Neil had obviously just come out of the shower—his hair was damp, and he was still doing up the buttons on his shirt. He was barefoot, and small droplets of water glistened on his perfectly muscled chest. Without thinking, Shefali put up a hand to touch his face. His skin was smooth and slightly damp, and she couldn't help leaning closer, until Neil took her wrist and drew her inside, shutting the door behind her. Neither of them spoke, just reaching out for each other blindly, and Neil's lips sought hers with a desperation that he didn't even try to hide.

Minutes later he drew away, cupping her face in his hands, his eyes troubled as he looked down into her eyes.

'I'm sorry,' he said. 'I didn't mean to grab you like that, but it was a surprise seeing you here and I lost my head a little.'

'So did I,' Shefali said, wondering how to continue.

She hadn't scripted this, and when she'd left home to come to Neil she hadn't even been sure if she was meeting him to finalise their break-up or attempt a reconciliation. Right now all she felt like doing was holding on to him and never letting him go.

'I'm so confused,' she blurted out suddenly, and then blushed in embarrassment. Great—so much for being in control and mature.

Neil didn't seem to think the remark gauche or immature, though. He released her and stepped back, pushing his hand through his rumpled hair. 'I know,' he said, smiling ruefully. 'We've made a bit of a pig's breakfast of this, between the two of us.'

Shefali could see what he meant, though she hadn't heard the expression before—it took her a few seconds to dispel the image of a porker nosing around in a vat of kitchen slops.

'So what do we do now?' she asked, hoping she sounded level-headed and rational, and wondering what she'd do if he suggested never seeing each other again.

'Let's sit down and talk it through,' he suggested. 'Sensibly. Keeping our hands off each other and everything. Bela and Nina have gone next door,' he added as Shefali looked around. 'We're alone.'

No incentive for keeping her hands off him, then.

Neil led the way into the dining room and they sat facing each other—as if they were at the United Nations, negotiating for world peace, Shefali thought a little hysterically.

'I'm sorry I upset you,' Neil said, and then there was a brief pause in which they stared wordlessly at each other.

'I can't understand why you feel the way you do,' Shefali said finally. 'But you're wonderful with Nina. I'd have thought you'd like the idea of a large family.'

'I didn't have a choice with Nina,' Neil said. 'I love her to bits. But becoming a father at twenty-four isn't something I'd recommend to anyone.'

Shefali opened her mouth to say something, but Neil leaned across the table and gripped her hand.

'I know I sound unreasonable,' he said. 'And I understand fully if you've decided you don't want to marry me after all. But try and think of it this way—what if you found out that I *couldn't* have children? What would you do?'

'Is that…?' Shefali said.

Neil shook his head. 'No,' he said. 'There's nothing wrong with me. Not physically at any rate.'

'No childhood attack of mumps?' Shefali said, trying to lighten the mood a little. 'Isn't that what it always is in books?'

Neil shook his head, his expression unchanged.

'It's not the same thing,' she protested. 'Not being able to have children is very different from deciding against having them.'

'But the decision that you need to take is essentially the same,' Neil said. 'Marrying me, knowing I'm not in favour of having another child—I'm not willing to take the risk for myself.'

'Right, so what if we agree on not having children until you're sure that our marriage will last?' Shefali said, striving to sound as emotionless as he did.

There was another long pause, and Shefali could see a vein throbbing at his temple as he held her gaze with his steady smoke-grey eyes.

'Why *do* you want to marry me?' she asked abruptly. 'Aren't I turning out to be more trouble than I'm worth?'

That got to him, she noted almost dispassionately, as Neil made a sudden movement of denial.

'Well?' she asked, her voice challenging, but something in his eyes made her stop and wait.

'I want to spend the rest of my life with you,' he said slowly, the words seemingly drawn out from him against his will. 'I care about you, and…'

'And?' she prompted, but her voice was softer now. Neil shut his eyes briefly. 'I can't give you everything you want,' he said, and his expression was bleak. 'It's only fair you have the chance to change your mind about marrying me. But if you do decide to go ahead with it I swear I'll try to make it up to you in every other way possible.'

He still hadn't said that he loved her, but for the first time Shefali felt she could live with the omission.

'Like I said, this isn't what I wanted,' she said quietly. 'But I love Nina, and I do want to marry you.'

At the last moment, her nerve failed her, and she wasn't able to tell him that she loved him too, but it didn't seem to matter. Neil was out of his chair in an instant, pulling her into his arms and holding her tightly, as if he never meant to let her go again.

* * *

Much later, when she was back home and getting ready to go to bed, the enormity of what she'd agreed to began to sink in. The sensible thing would have been to cut her losses and leave, rather than condemn herself to a lifetime of loving a man who didn't love her back. But she was stupidly and irrevocably in love with Neil, and pretty much any kind of compromise seemed accept-able when the alternative was spending the rest of her life without him.

Telling Neil that she didn't want to marry him would have been pretty much like taking a butcher's cleaver to her limbs—she'd never have been able to do it. She'd just have to figure out how to manage with what he was offering her and hope that he'd change his mind about having children. Or that a man who'd been careless enough to get one woman pregnant by accident would repeat the mistake.

Smiling grimly at the thought, she finally fell asleep at around four a.m. and woke up with a start when her alarm rang three hours later.

CHAPTER ELEVEN

NEIL LEFT FOR Mumbai a few days later. Shefali was to join him in three weeks. As it turned out there was a vacancy in the Mumbai office of the playschool which was coming up around then. Also, Mrs Dubey was getting rather bored in Pune, and was more than happy to come out of retirement and return to Jabalpur to manage the school.

'Frankly, I expected this would happen,' Shefali's boss told her when she rang the day she was leaving for Mumbai. 'Mrs Dubey's not the kind to sit around in Pune keeping house for her son, and I knew you wouldn't want to be in Jabalpur for more than a few months.'

'But when I moved here I was planning to stay on for a few years at least,' Shefali protested. 'It's just that I met Neil and…'

'If it hadn't been Neil it would have been someone else,' her boss said cheerfully. 'Or you'd have gone back to your parents. Now, are you going to stick at this Mumbai job or not?'

'Of course I am,' she said. 'I'm just trying to figure out how far the school is from Neil's flat.' She typed both addresses into the internet—seven kilometers apart, the application informed her cheerily. 'That's not very close, is it?' she asked, frowning at the screen.

'It's close enough by Mumbai standards,' her boss said. 'And you can put your step-daughter in the same school, so you won't have to worry about her while you're at work.'

'She's joining regular school this month,' Shefali said. 'I'll ring off, Shwetank. I need to leave soon. Thanks for everything.'

Step-daughter. It was the first time Shefali had heard anyone use the word for Nina, and it sounded cold and not quite real—as if Nina had just stepped out of the pages of *Snow White* or *Cinderella*. They'd decided to take things slowly at the beginning, to allow Nina to get used to the idea of having a 'new mother', but Nina would have none of it, insisting on calling Shefali Mamma as soon as the engagement was announced. Reema was still 'Mum', and Nina seemed to be handling the distinction very well.

Shefali sighed as she heaved her bags onto the train. There was a fairly big contingent of people at the station to see her off—Mrs Dubey and most of the staff from the school, and quite a few tiny tots with their mums. She found herself getting a little teary-eyed as she waved to them from the steps as the train pulled out of the station, and she splashed a little water on her face before going to her seat in the first-class section. There was an elderly couple sharing her carriage, and she buried her face in a magazine to avoid being drawn into conversation.

With the wedding just two days away, Shefali was in serious danger of succumbing to an attack of pre-wedding nerves. There were, of course, various reminders of the previous time she'd almost got married—the elderly and slightly eccentric aunt who'd called to ask if she'd mind if she was given the gift originally bought for her wedding to Pranav; the friend from the US who'd not heard about the break-up and was genuinely perplexed when she got an invitation for a second wedding. Even the tussle with her mother over what to wear for the reception had had nasty little undertones of 'last time I did what you said, and look what happened'.

But worse than that was her fear of things not working out. She was worrying about a million things. Whether Neil would ever change his mind about having children, whether they'd be compatible, even whether Nina would accept her or not. Pretty much everyone who had heard about the wedding seemed to think that teaching kindergarten for three years was completely inadequate preparation for step-motherhood. And now there was a bunch of new fears that hadn't even occurred to her earlier—what if Reema turned Nina against her? What if Neil objected when she tried to discipline Nina? What if she couldn't get along with Neil's parents? In a way, her fears helped her stave off the worst demon of them all—that Neil didn't love her. He'd never said he did. She'd just assumed that he must, given that he was marrying her in spite of all his misgivings. Maybe she'd been wrong all along?

The thought kept cropping up at regular intervals, like a spectre at a feast, and she tried to distract herself with magazines and details of the wedding ceremony Barbara Mitra had sent her.

She was still worrying twenty hours later as the train pulled into the erstwhile Victoria Terminus. The station was now called the Chhatrapati Shivaji Terminus, after a famous Maratha warrior, she recalled, and tried to remember what he was famous for—fighting the British? The Mughals? Her history was weak at the best of times, and she had an unconscious phobia for all things related to Mumbai. Born and bred in Delhi, she had absorbed some of the true Delhi-ite's discomfort at the bustling, business-driven life on the island city.

It was a bright, sunny morning, but the condensation on the tinted windows of the air-conditioned train made it difficult to see out, and she couldn't spot Neil anywhere on the platform. Disappointment clouded her eyes as the train ground to a halt and she still didn't see him. Maybe he'd got delayed, or was waiting at the wrong section of the platform? She started putting her things together, wondering if she should call him before she got off the train. She'd turned to peer out of the window one last time when the door of her compartment slid open.

'Looking for someone?' a familiar voice asked, and she whirled around to see Neil standing at the doorway.

Shefali jumped to her feet with an incoherent little cry and flung herself into his arms, hugging him fiercely. The elderly couple had got off at Dadar, so there was no one else in the carriage—Neil stepped in and shut the door behind him, crushing her lips under his in a kiss that had several weeks' worth of pent-up desire in it.

'God, I've missed you,' he said throatily when they finally came up for air. 'It feels like years since I held you last.'

Shefali leaned her head against his chest for a few minutes, breathing in the fresh, clean scent of his skin, too overwhelmed to speak. Her doubts had receded into the background the instant she'd set eyes on Neil, but now she was in the throes of a serious case of lust.

'Come on—let's get out of here,' Neil said. 'We have a couple of hours before the rest of my family descends on us—let's make the most of it.'

He picked up her bags and got off the train, turning around to swing her down into his arms.

'Travelling light this time, I see,' he said teasingly. Most of her luggage had gone on ahead, and she had only a couple of cases with her.

'Just stuff to last me till the wedding,' she said. 'My mum's bringing a truckload of things from Delhi, though.'

She couldn't keep her eyes off Neil. As usual he was dressed in jeans and a white shirt, and he looked good enough to eat. He'd had a haircut, and she couldn't help reaching up and ruffling his hair.

He took her hand and pressed a quick kiss into the palm. 'I've booked you into a hotel,' he said, and, in answer to her unspoken question, 'I'm staying there as well—for tonight at least. I wanted us to have some time with each other before the wedding, especially since our honeymoon's not for a while.'

Their honeymoon had had to be delayed because Nina had got a mid-term vacancy at a rather swanky South Mumbai school and would be joining immediately after the wedding. Neil wasn't comfortable with being out of town while she was settling down, so they'd decided to push forward their trip to the Maldives by a month.

'How's Nina?' Shefali asked, as Neil's driver put the luggage into Neil's SUV.

'Excited,' he said briefly. 'That's the other reason

for the hotel—she's not likely to give you a minute to breathe if you stay with us.'

Shefali scooted a little closer to Neil, wanting to touch him again but very conscious of the driver's presence in the car. Evidently not troubled by such scruples, Neil tipped her face up for a scorching hot kiss.

'Not here,' she mumbled, trying to push him away, but she succumbed as soon as his lips touched hers.

She cast an embarrassed look at the front seat when Neil finally released her, but the driver was looking straight ahead, his face impassive. Obviously he was discreet, and Shefali couldn't help wondering if he was used to his boss kissing women in the back seat of the car. A little shaft of jealousy shot through her. They hadn't talked about it, but since his divorce it was unlikely that Neil had stayed celibate. And he must meet attractive women all the time in his line of work...

'You're frowning,' Neil remarked, leaning back against the headrest. 'Something wrong?'

'No, I was just thinking that there's a lot to be done if we're getting married tomorrow...'

'Everything's done,' Neil said easily. 'We're getting married in the registry office, and the reception is at the same hotel you're staying at. I called in a few favours and got a booking at short notice. And Rafiq and Priti pitched in to organise the decorations and the cake.'

He took in her tense expression. She'd clearly used the wedding arrangements as a blind, but now she seemed *really* worried at the casual way Neil seemed to be taking everything.

'Relax,' he said. 'Nothing will go wrong. Rafiq and I have organised events for ten times the number of people in half the time. And those were being telecast live.'

'So a wedding reception is small change for you guys?' Shefali muttered, remembering the months her mother had slaved over the tiniest details of the arrangements for her first wedding.

Neil laughed and leaned across to kiss her again. 'Absolutely,' he said.

There was a half-mocking, half-caressing note in his voice that made Shefali murmur, 'Just you wait till I get you alone.'

'Another ten minutes,' he said huskily, deliberately misinterpreting the remark, and the sensual promise in his voice sent pleasurable shivers up Shefali's spine.

It took less than ten minutes to reach the hotel, but checking in took some time, and then the bellboy insisted on showing them to their suite and explaining how all the TV and air-conditioning controls worked.

'I think we'll figure it out,' Shefali interrupted, taking two hundred-rupee notes out her purse and putting them into the young man's hand.

He took them, but didn't leave the room. 'Ma'am, I need to tell you where the fire escapes are,' he said earnestly.

'Isn't there a map or something I can look at?'

'Ma'am, it's the hotel's safety policy. I need to explain in person.'

Neil was openly laughing as he threw himself into an armchair, and Shefali glared at him as the bellboy painstakingly explained where each and every emergency exit was. Shefali hoped devoutly that Neil was paying attention—the boy could have been giving her the floor plan for the Prince of Wales Museum for all the sense she could make of it.

'Thanks,' she said when he wound to a close.

He wasn't done, though. 'Ma'am, if you need to order from Room Service…'

'If I do, I'll look the number up in the hotel directory,' Shefali said firmly, and glanced at the man's name tag. 'Thanks a lot, Ahmed, you've been really helpful. But I've not seen my fiancé for three weeks—' she gestured towards Neil '—and I really, really want to spend some time alone with him.'

'Yes—of course, ma'am,' Ahmed said, blushing a fetching shade of pink and scuttling out of the room.

Shefali shut the door behind him and latched it firmly, then took the phone off the hook. She walked very deliberately across to Neil and started unbuttoning his shirt. She was very, very careful till the third button, doing the task as slowly and seductively as possible, then she said, 'Ah—what the hell? I hope you aren't too fond of this shirt.' And ripped it off him, sending buttons flying across the room.

Before her hands could reach his jeans he had picked her up, putting her on the bed in one fluid movement and looming over her as he swiftly divested her of her clothes.

Happily, Shefali let him take over—Neil was wonderful when he was being masterful—and her mouth fell open in a helpless little 'oh' of delight as he covered her body with his and proceeded to make ruthless love to her.

Afterwards, he gently ran a hand over the silken lines of her body. 'I was planning a rather grand seduction,' he said ruefully. 'But it sort of slipped my mind back here.'

Shefali took a swig from the bottle of water she'd taken out of the mini-bar and scooted closer to him.

'Don't worry—you did well,' she said, patting his arm consolingly. 'I'd give you a five out of ten.'

'Five?' Neil asked, outraged. 'I'd say seven at least.'

Shefali thought it over. 'OK, I'll give you a seven,' she conceded. 'But I'll need to see the grand seduction routine tonight.' She caught sight of her watch and said, 'Oh, help! Weren't we supposed to meet your parents at your place at three?'

'They'll understand,' Neil said lazily.

'That's exactly what I'm worried about,' Shefali said, bouncing out of bed and pulling on her clothes in a hurry. 'Come on,' she said, slinging a pillow at him. 'Let's go meet the family.'

Neil groaned, but he got out of bed. Shefali was right. They needed to leave. Even though all he wanted right now was to pull her back into bed and make love to her for the rest of the day. But his parents and his sister would have arrived at his flat, and Nina was impatient to see Shefali as well. He'd just have to wait till tonight to get Shefali to himself again.

On the way to Neil's South Mumbai flat he pointed out the school where Shefali would be working.

'Is Nina's school nearby?' she asked.

'Opposite direction,' Neil said. 'The school's near Marine Drive.'

Shefali thought for a bit. 'Would it make sense for me to try for a job in her school?' she asked. 'Then we could travel together, and it'd be easier for me to keep a track of what's happening with her.'

'I think you should stay where you are,' Neil said. 'My mum was a teacher in the school I went to and, boy, did it take the fun out of life! I'd get punished twice for every darn thing I did in school once by the teacher, and once by my mum when she found out what had happened.'

Shefali laughed, but she found it oddly comforting that Neil wasn't expecting her to be with Nina twenty-four seven. That was one of the many barbs that had struck home—the suggestion that he was marrying her just because he thought she'd make a younger and better-qualified nanny for Nina than Bela. She didn't really believe it, but once in a while insecurities did creep in.

Barbara Mitra came up to give Shefali a warm hug as soon as she stepped into the flat. Shefali smiled at the tiny blonde woman with genuine affection. Barbara was efficient, motherly and down-to-earth—as different from Shefali's own socialite mother as possible—and in her neat cotton sari with her hair done up in a bun she looked far more like the embodiment of traditional Indian values than Mrs Khanna. Shefali's mother wouldn't be seen dead in anything less glamorous than silks and chiffons.

'We have a crisis on our hands,' Barbara announced. 'Nina's not happy with the outfit you got her, Neil.'

Neil frowned. '*She* chose it,' he said, looking across at his daughter. 'After dragging me across half a dozen shops. What's wrong now, Nina?'

'You got me the wrong kind of beads!' Nina wailed. 'I meant the kind that go in your *hair*! Why couldn't you have asked Mamma Shefali? She'd have *known*. She's not a dumb man like you!'

'Nina!' Barbara and Shefali said at the same time, and Nina scowled.

'Sorry,' she said to her father, clearly not sorry at all. 'But I explained to him what I wanted and now I'll not look nice at the wedding and it's all *his* fault.'

'Clearly,' Neil said, looking more amused than annoyed. 'Should I take you to the shops with me now, pumpkin? Or should we delay the wedding till we find you the correct hair accessories?'

'I'll go and get them,' Shefali said. 'I think I know what she wants.'

'Rose-pink and dark pink,' Nina ordered.

For a second Shefali wanted to smack her. Then good sense re-asserted itself. It was difficult for a four-year-old to cope with anyone else being the focus of attention, and if Nina was acting uncharacteristically bratty it was probably because she was as stressed about the wedding as Shefali was herself.

'Rose-pink and dark pink it is,' she said, and Nina's lovely little face broke into such a happy smile that Shefali felt her heart go out to her. She smiled back at her and, leaning down, gave her a little hug.

'Your friends from your old school made a card for you,' she said. 'And I've got you a couple of gifts as well—I'll give them to you once I get back from the store.'

'I'll take you,' Neil said. 'There's a store ten minutes from here.'

Shefali was beginning to get her bearings around the area—the store was in the same direction as her hotel—but she was glad to have Neil by her side, pointing out landmarks and explaining the road signs which seemed to be designed to confuse.

'This place reminds me of my grandparents,' Neil said as he pushed open the door of the store. 'I used to go to London every summer, and the original version of this store is right next to their house. My grandmother used to spoil me silly, buying me stuff from there. In those days you didn't get the same kind of stuff in India. I think I was more thrilled than Nina was when they opened a branch here.'

'It's pretty amazing,' Shefali agreed, going across to the girls' clothing section and rummaging through a large bin of hair accessories. 'These are the kind she wants,' she said, clipping open some of the beads and showing Neil how they would fit over a braid.

Neil was investigating a shelf full of dolls.

'Do you think Nina would like one of these?' he asked. 'That Dora of hers is getting rather ratty. But these look awful. They're anorexic. Except for that one—*ugh*, it's pregnant!' he recoiled from a row of dolls sporting prominent baby bumps. 'Why would they sell those things to little kids?' he asked in appalled tones as they paid for the beads and left the store.

Shefali shrugged. 'I guess it's supposed to be a way to help a kid deal with her mum expecting a child. I don't know. Look, I'm dying for a cup of coffee—do we have time?'

'We do,' Neil said, leading the way into a small café near the store.

Evidently the pregnant doll was still playing on Neil's mind, because after ordering their coffees he said, 'Bringing up a girl is a lot tougher than bringing up a boy. I wouldn't have known how to explain those dolls if Nina had been with me. Some of this stuff is positively embarrassing when it's your own daughter you're talking to.'

'Aren't you glad I'm going to be around?' Shefali asked teasingly.

'It's a big relief,' he admitted. 'Every time I used to think of Nina reaching her teens I'd break into a cold sweat—my mother and sister are in different cities, and Bela Mashi's not likely to be clued in about stuff like clothes and make-up and Lord knows what else.'

'Trainer bras,' Shefali supplied. 'And boyfriends. And vampire movies. And tattoos. And whether facial piercing is a good idea.'

Neil blanched. 'You can handle all that, thank you very much,' he said. 'I wouldn't know what to do.'

'Yes, of course,' Shefali said, but she couldn't help thinking how unfair it was. Neil was expecting her to treat his child as her own when he refused even to consider having children with her.

Some of her feelings must have shown on her face, because Neil reached across the table and took her hands in his. 'Nervous about the wedding?' he asked softly.

Shefali looked up. At that same moment a baby began to cry somewhere in the café, and quite suddenly something seemed to snap within her. 'Yes,' she said. 'And not just about the wedding. I'm nervous about a lot.'

His eyebrows arched up in query, and Shefali stood up clumsily.

'Let's get out of here,' she muttered.

The coffee was already paid for, and Neil had her out of the café in a few minutes.

'What's wrong?' he asked quietly.

'I can't not have children of my own,' Shefali said, as the doubts and fears of the last few weeks crystallised into one inescapable fact. 'I don't know why I agreed to it. I can't marry you—we'll have to call off the wedding.'

Neil absorbed the statement slowly, his grey-blue

eyes not wavering from her face as she looked up at him helplessly.

'What's brought this on?' he asked. 'When you got off the train this morning you seemed perfectly OK, and afterwards...'

Afterwards she'd been so blinded by her feelings for Neil that she'd determinedly pushed every doubt out of her mind. Even now the impulse to capitulate and throw herself into his arms was immense. Her nails dug into her palms as she clenched her hands, willing herself not to move closer to him.

'I'm sorry,' she said, her face pale and miserable. 'I've been trying to tell myself that this will work, but it won't.'

'Is this just about having children?' Neil asked. 'Because if it is...'

'It's not just that,' Shefali said. 'Though that's the biggest reason.'

'What else, then?'

Shefali made a despairing gesture. 'You didn't want to get involved with me in the first place. Ever since we started seeing each other it's like I've been pushing you into taking the next step—you've always been reluctant.'

Neil started to say something, but Shefali forestalled him.

'It's my fault,' she said. 'I was on the rebound from Pranav, and I... I...' Even now she couldn't bring herself to admit that she loved Neil, so she said instead, 'I was so keen on marrying you I agreed to whatever you said. I didn't stop to think what our lives would be like after we'd married—'

'There will be absolutely nothing wrong with our

lives after we marry,' Neil interrupted, his heart thudding so loudly he could hardly hear himself speak.

The thought of losing Shefali was unbearable. He'd taken it for granted, assumed he'd have all the time in the world to reverse his decision about starting a family with her—and now, already, it seemed it might be too late.

'I've had a lot of time to think ever since I got back to Mumbai and you're right,' he said. 'It's not fair to you, insisting that we don't have children. Hell, it's probably not even fair to Nina—you'd be unhappy, and you'd start resenting her after a while, and that's the last thing she needs.'

'Are you saying you've changed your mind?' she said slowly.

'I have,' he said, bitterly regretting the old habit of caution that had stopped him from telling her sooner. 'We can have as many kids you want. I was being impractical and wrong-headed before. And as far as the rest of it goes, I've said it many times—I've always wanted to be with you. If I've pulled back at times it's because I thought it was best either for you or for Nina…'

And I love you, he thought. *I can't live without you.* But the words stuck in his throat when he tried to say them. The realisation of what she meant to him had come late, and he needed some time to get to grips with the emotions that were sweeping over him.

'Right…' Shefali said, her eyes searching his face for a clue as to how he really felt.

He held her gaze, taking her hand and bringing it up to his lips. 'We'll be great together,' he said softly. 'Trust me.'

'How do I know you won't change your mind again?' she asked finally.

'I won't,' he said, and there was enough conviction in his tone for her to finally accept what he was saying.

He still hadn't told her he loved her, but she didn't have the guts to push the point. He cared deeply for her, that much was evident, and it would have to do.

'The wedding goes ahead as planned, then?' he asked, and she nodded.

She felt drained and a little sick after the emotional rollercoaster of the last fifteen minutes.

'I guess,' Shefali said, and her voice was subdued. The incident felt like a preview of the rest of her life with Neil. She'd always be on guard, always be apologising for saying the wrong thing. He would brush her apologies aside, but inside he'd be wondering why he'd married her. 'Can you drop me back at the hotel?' she asked. 'I'm really tired. And, Neil…?'

'You don't want me to come back with you?' he said.

She nodded. 'I'm really tired,' she said again, and he didn't object.

His sense of relief after the averted crisis was immense, but he knew that there was a long way to go before he and Shefali reached the level of understanding they needed for a successful marriage. Right now he was just profoundly grateful that they were getting married at all, after the hash he had made of things.

'I'll see you tomorrow,' Shefali said as the car pulled up in front of the hotel. On a sudden impulse she leaned across and kissed Neil hard on the mouth, slipping out of the car and running up the hotel steps without turning back to look at him.

Once in her room, she collapsed into bed and fell

fast asleep, waking only when her mother called her the next morning to demand whether she was ready for the registry office wedding.

The wedding ceremony itself was rather dire, performed in a dingy little office at the civil court. Shefali was dressed in a simple but expensive *khadi* silk sari, and she looked as out of place among the bored clerks and pairs of runaway lovebirds as a swan in a congregation of crows.

'What a way to get married,' her mother remarked disgustedly as they finally exited the court. 'It hardly seems legal.'

'It's perfectly legal, Mum,' Shefali said wearily. 'Actually, it's a sight more legal than going through a religious ceremony and forgetting to register it afterwards, like Shravan.'

Her older brother had had a tough time getting his marriage legalised when he'd realised that the last date for registering it had gone by. His wife had been expecting their first child, and she'd gone mental when she'd realised that the baby would be deemed illegitimate unless the paperwork was sorted out.

Her mother gave a ladylike snort. 'I hope the reception party is a little more civilised,' she said, changing the subject as she always did when she didn't like the direction a conversation was taking.

Shefali was dreading the wedding reception. It was to be a smallish affair by Delhi standards, but there would still be over two hundred people attending, mainly relatives and friends. She'd expected the occasion to be a happy one, but now she couldn't wait for it to be over.

'Who's doing your hair and make-up?' her mother demanded, following her to her hotel room.

Her parents were in the same hotel as she was—so was Shravan, with his wife and now-legitimate son—and her mother was rapidly trying to assume control over the arrangements.

'I don't know. Rafiq and Priti are sending someone.'

Her mother looked deeply suspicious. 'What kind of someone?' she demanded. 'I hope it's not one of those roadside beauty parlour types. I *knew* I should have brought Shabnam down with me from Delhi. She did such a wonderful job with your wedding make-up last time. You looked like a princess.' Noticing Shefali's expression, she said, 'It's not *her* fault the wedding got called off. And she *understands* your hair and skin. Someone new might make a hash of things.'

Shefali wished she could tell her mother that right now she could do with some understanding of herself, but she bit the words back. Her mother would throw a hissy fit if she knew that things between her and Neil weren't as hunky-dory as they seemed. And her father had prudently removed himself from the whole hair and make-up discussion—he'd arranged to meet some former colleagues at the bar before the reception began.

Not even Shefali's mother could find fault with the stylist when he finally arrived—Freddy Contractor was the make-up man for one of Bollywood's leading ladies, and had his own extremely popular TV show. Rafiq had shamelessly traded favours to get him to come.

He took a long look at Shefali. 'This won't do,' he said finally.

Shefali gave herself a nervous look in the mirror. What wouldn't do? Her clothes, her hair, her face—what?

Freddy leaned closer to her, his breath smelling of

mint and cloves. 'You don't look happy,' he whispered
in her ear. 'Today's supposed to be the happiest day of
your life. You should be smiling all the time, but you're
looking so depressed. What's the matter? Had a fight
with Neil?'

Oh, God, of course he'd know Neil—they both did
shows for the same channel.

'Something like that,' she muttered, too low for her
mother to catch.

'So the best way to get back at him is to look so sexy
that you knock his socks off,' Freddy said briskly. 'And
he turns into your willing slave.'

This, unfortunately, did reach Mrs Khanna's ears,
and she looked terribly scandalised—Shefali, on the
other hand, giggled involuntarily.

'Hmm, *muuuch* better,' Freddy said approvingly.
'Now, if you could just tilt your head back a little…'

The whole getting ready business took a good three
hours—Freddy wasn't happy with the way Mrs Khanna
draped Shefali's sari the first two times, and only when
he threatened to rip it off and redrape it himself did
she follow his instructions to the letter. Her make-up
was perfect—very light, with just enough eyeliner and
shadow to accentuate her undeniably beautiful eyes,
and a little bit of blush and glitter to add colour to her
pale cheeks. Freddy had figured out early on that Mrs
Khanna was a celebrity hound, and at any sign of her
wanting to interfere he dropped a few names and she
backed off.

'Now for your hair,' he said, and carefully started removing the rollers he'd put it into. Then he went to work
with tongs and hairspray, and soon had Shefali's hair
cascading down in a mass of soft ringlets. He frowned

and shook his head at the first set of gemstone-encrusted pins Mrs Khanna offered him. 'Ah—those are perfect,' he said, taking simple plain gold clips from her and pinning back Shefali's hair at the sides. 'So what do you think?' he asked, swivelling Shefali's chair around so that she could look at herself in the mirror.

'She looks beautiful,' Mrs Khanna conceded grudgingly. 'Though I think the *bindi* could have been a little bigger.'

'Shefali?'

Shefali was still inspecting herself.

'I'll knock his socks off,' she said with quiet confidence, and this time Freddy burst into laughter.

'Way to go, girl,' he said approvingly. He lowered his voice as Mrs Khanna left the room with one of his assistants to get her own make-up and hair touched up. 'You want to talk about it, let me know. Hairdressers' code of honour—we never tell.'

Shefali shook her head, smiling. 'No, that wouldn't be fair to Neil. But thanks, Freddy.' She leaned up to kiss him on the cheek, and Neil chose exactly that moment to walk into the suite.

He was brought up short by the sight of his bride in another man's arms. 'Am I interrupting something?' he asked stiffly. Industry gossip said that Freddy was gay, but Neil had always had his doubts. And, gay or not gay, Shefali was standing far too close to him for Neil's liking.

'Oh, not at all,' Freddy said smoothly, gathering up his things. 'We were just talking about…socks.'

'Socks?' Neil said, not even trying to keep the scepticism out of his voice.

'Yes, well, Freddy thinks they won't…go with the

whole sari look,' Shefali said, and both she and Freddy burst into fresh laughter.

'People have started arriving,' Neil said when they'd stopped. 'If you're ready, shall we go down?'

'Yes, of course,' Shefali said, standing up and slipping on her heels.

She gave Neil a quick look. He was wearing a dark grey suit that perfectly moulded his powerful shoulders and lean physique, and he looked magnificent—though his expression wasn't happy. She was about to say something when Freddy spoke.

'Looking good, man,' he said, leaning across to adjust Neil's tie by a fraction. 'Now, just a minute.' He grabbed Shefali's hand and pulled her away from Neil to spray a cloud of perfume into the air. 'Walk through that,' he ordered, and she complied while Neil backed away to avoid getting any on himself.

'Ready to roll,' Freddy said, and Shefali walked out of the suite with Neil.

The reception was to be in the ballroom on the first floor of the hotel, and they'd have to take the lift down. Freddy was still packing up his make-up bag, so they were alone in the lift.

'You look beautiful,' Neil said quietly as the doors slid shut. 'I'm sorry. That's the first thing I should have said.'

'Not too bad yourself,' Shefali said, though her heart was hammering so loudly in her chest she was surprised he couldn't hear it. She let her eyes rest for a few seconds on his face. His eyes looked tired, as if he hadn't slept very well, and on impulse she put a hand up to his cheek. 'Cheer up,' she said softly.

He groaned, his hands coming up to grip her shoulders. 'Don't,' he said, unconsciously echoing Freddy. 'This is supposed to be the happiest day of our lives—we shouldn't need cheering up.'

A ghost of a smile flitted across Shefali's lips. 'I'm sorry I ran out on you yesterday,' she said. 'I thought it over later and—well, let's just try and take each day as it comes, shall we? We'll be happy together. I'm sure of it.'

Neil didn't answer directly but he pressed a button to stop the lift and bent down to kiss her, his lips hot and demanding against hers. 'I don't deserve you,' he said when he finally let her go, her face flushed, and her make-up a little smudged. 'But I'll do my damnedest to make you happy.'

Did that mean he'd definitely changed his mind about children? Shefali wondered as the lift doors slid open. Or just that he'd do everything else he could to keep her happy?

She automatically plastered a smile on her face as the first set of guests came across to meet them.

Freddy soon hurried across to her. 'Shefali, your make-up!' he scolded. 'I told you you'd knock his socks off, didn't I?'

She smiled at him as he opened his bag and started dabbing at her mouth with a ball of cotton. 'So you did,' she said.

'Things better?' he asked softly.

She shook her head, a lone tear escaping from her eye and sliding down her cheek. 'Not really,' she said. It wasn't something she'd easily admit, but Freddy had got past her defences effortlessly.

Freddy grabbed a glass from a passing waiter's tray. 'Drink this,' he said firmly. 'I cannot, repeat, *cannot* have you leaking mascara all over the place.'

Shefali took a swig. He was right, it did help, and she drained the rest of the glass quickly.

'Is that alcoholic?' a shocked voice said.

She turned to see her mother standing right behind her and nodded defiantly.

'You're *drinking* at your own wedding reception?' her mother continued.

'She probably just needs a shot of Dutch courage before she meets the family,' Barbara Mitra said, coming up to Shefali and giving her arm a reassuring squeeze. 'Come on—let me introduce you to everyone.'

'There's no stage,' Mrs Khanna said, sounding annoyed. 'Normally they would sit on the stage and everyone would come and meet them there—at least that's the way it's done in Delhi.'

'I don't think they do it that way in Mumbai,' Shefali said, stifling a giggle. The wine had gone to her head rather quickly.

'And there's no videographer either,' Mrs Khanna said, sounding even more upset.

Rafiq caught the last remark. '*Arrey*, Aunty, what to do? I told Neil but he said he didn't want any *tamasha*...'

Rafiq's approach to Shefali's mother was the opposite to Freddy's—he agreed fervently with everything she said, thereby immediately antagonising everyone else within earshot.

'Come, Nina's been waiting to see you,' Barbara said, and drew Shefali away.

Nina was standing with a slim woman who looked so much like her that Shefali didn't need an introduction. She'd expected to feel animosity towards her, but Reema was so natural and unaffected that she found herself actually liking her.

Neil looked across the room and saw Shefali and Reema together. He winced. His mother belonged to the 'if there's an elephant in the room introduce it' school of thought, which Neil subscribed to in theory but not in practice. Ideally he would have liked it if Reema hadn't come, but she was Nina's mother, and their parents were still friends—families bound together by their common grandchild.

'Excuse me,' Neil said to the colleagues he was standing with, and strode across the open terrace to Shefali's side.

'Shefali Mamma, you're not wearing *mehandi* this time,' Nina was exclaiming in disappointment. 'You wore it last time, when—'

'Nina, that's enough,' Neil said sharply, and both Shefali and Reema turned in surprise.

'Whoa—no longer the super-indulgent Daddy, I see,' Reema said teasingly, but when Neil's expression turned thunderous she put out a hand in appeasement. 'Sorry, sorry—just saying.'

'Hi, Reema,' Neil said curtly. 'Just got here?'

'Some time ago, actually. I was with Barbara and Nina.' She paused, then said a little self-consciously but very sincerely, 'Congratulations, Neil. I'm so happy for both of you.'

She meant it, Shefali thought wonderingly as she looked at Reema. She genuinely wanted Neil to be happy.

Neil seemed to realise it too, and he smiled down at Reema, his expression much warmer. 'Thank you,' he said. 'I see you've already met Shefali.'

'Yes, and she's lovely,' Reema said. 'Relax, Neil, we're not going to have a cat-fight. You didn't need to come charging to the rescue. I think we might even end up being friends. Especially if Shefali tells me the story behind no *mehandi*—I'm dying of curiosity.'

She gave both of them a sunny little smile, and Neil groaned. There was a reason why Barbara and Reema had always got on so well—neither of them believed in being discreet.

'I almost got married once before,' Shefali said. 'And I'd had my hands covered with *mehandi* designs. The wedding didn't happen, but Nina met me soon afterwards and she remembers them.'

'I think we need to circulate a little,' Neil said abruptly. 'I'll see you around, Reema. Nina, are you staying with your mum?'

'Yes,' Nina said happily. 'She's telling me about the stuff she's got me from the US.'

'She seems nice,' Shefali ventured when they were out of earshot.

Neil shrugged. 'She's all right,' he said. 'I don't like seeing her with Nina, that's all.'

That was understandable, Shefali thought, and she gave Neil's arm a quick squeeze. Given that Reema hadn't wanted the child initially, and after she was born hadn't wanted to have anything to do with her, it must be difficult to see Nina being so friendly with her now.

The band struck up an old Bollywood number, and several couples stepped onto the dance floor.

'Aren't you two dancing?' Neil's father asked them in mock horror, and they found themselves being pushed onto the dance floor.

Neil was a good dancer—perhaps because his mother had taught him. Shefali found herself following his lead with practically no effort, and for the first time that evening she relaxed and began to enjoy herself. The feel of Neil's arms around her was utter bliss, and on the dance floor he seemed less tense as well, smiling deep into her eyes as he twirled her in time to the music.

The song came to an end, and people near them clapped.

'May I?' Mr Mitra said, and led Shefali back on to the floor.

After that she danced with Shravan and Rafiq and Freddy, laughing as they swung her around boisterously, her hair flying over her flushed face.

Neil had stepped off the dance floor and was watching quietly from the terrace when a small hand slipped into his. Nina didn't look up at him, though. She had eyes only for Shefali.

'She dances so *well*,' Nina said, and Neil nodded.

It had just struck him that Shefali looked happier now than she had since she'd set foot in Mumbai—perhaps happier than he'd ever seen her before. And no credit to him. It was probably just the music, and she was letting herself go, letting herself laugh and have fun.

'She's amazing,' a voice said next to him, and he turned to Reema, an unconscious frown on his face. Nina slipped off to find Bela Mashi, and they were alone together.

'I know,' he said.

'Nina's so fond of her, and your parents are crazy about her,' Reema continued, ignoring the frown on his face. 'And you're a completely different person now.'

'I am?' he asked, unable to keep the surprise out of his face.

'Of course you are, Neil!' Reema turned to him. 'You used to be obsessed with Nina, and you were working yourself into the ground, you had casual, meaningless flings, but no serious relationships—now it's like you've finally found your moorings.'

'Quite the little psychoanalyst,' Neil said sarcastically.

Reema flushed. 'I'm not trying to be patronising,' she said. 'We've known each other all our lives, Neil. Sometimes it feels like I know you better than I know myself. We were best friends, but we should never have married each other—what we had was boy-girl stuff. It was sweet, but it would have blown over and we'd have gone back to being friends. What you have now is the real thing.'

She fell silent, and Neil, feeling his heart beating faster, said, 'What d'you mean, "the real thing"?'

'Both of you are obviously head over heels in love with each other,' she said, adding with a little gurgle of laughter, 'Even Nina can see it.'

'Thanks,' Neil said absently.

Even Nina could see it—but they hadn't yet actually acknowledged their feelings for each other. He'd been mired in his own hang-ups and so had Shefali, probably. Unless he was wrong, and Shefali didn't love him after all. His heart twisted within him at the thought, and he squared his shoulders unconsciously, as if he were readying himself for a blow. There was only one way to find out, he thought, crossing the ballroom with purposeful strides. Freddy was still twirling Shefali in his arms, and Neil tapped him on the shoulder.

'I'd like my wife back, please,' he said, and Freddy relinquished her without a peep.

'Socks!' he called out cheekily, as Shefali followed Neil off the dance floor.

She looked up at Neil in concern. 'Is everything OK?' she asked.

'Everything's perfect,' he said. 'I just need to talk to you for a few minutes. Alone,' he added as she stood there expectantly.

No one noticed them leave the ballroom except Reema, and she didn't draw attention to it.

Neil took Shefali into a small room next to the ballroom that was being used to store the gifts and bouquets. Once inside, he shut the door behind him and took her hands into his.

'This mightn't be what you want to hear from me right now,' he said, 'but I couldn't not tell you.' At the startled look on her face, he smiled slightly and said, 'Relax, it's nothing terrible. And before I begin I just want to say I don't really have any expectations. I mean, I don't want you to feel obliged to....'

He saw the confused look on Shefali's face, and said, 'Damn, I'm making a mess of this. I only want to tell you that...' He took a deep breath. 'That I love you.' Shefali's eyes widened, and he went on hurriedly, 'I know you mightn't feel the same about me, but I'm hoping that with time you will. And even if you don't that's—'

He broke off abruptly as tears welled into Shefali's eyes.

'What did I say?' he asked worriedly. 'Sweetheart, don't cry. We can forget about this. It's not—'

'You big idiot,' Shefali wailed, throwing herself into his arms. 'I've been in love with you for months, and months, I've been through hell. Neil, do you really mean it?'

A big weight seemed to have lifted off Neil's shoulders, and he felt years younger as he gently cupped her face in his hands.

'I really, really mean it,' he said, kissing her tear-stained face very, very gently, as if she was the most precious thing in the entire universe. 'I love you, and I always will. I'm sorry I didn't tell you earlier, but I promise I'll spend the rest of my life making it up to you.'

'I love you too,' she said, smiling mistily up at him. 'And—oh, Neil, do we really need to go back and see all those people again? I know it's our wedding reception...'

'No, we don't need to go back,' he said, and he took her arm and walked her quickly to the elevators.

A few stray guests gave them curious looks—Shefali's make-up was irretrievably smeared now—but there were stars in her eyes, and she was so evidently, radiantly happy that everyone who saw her smiled involuntarily.

Back in their suite, Neil made such slow, delicious love to her, practically worshipping her with his body, that her eyes filled with tears again. He kissed them away gently, and afterwards she lay quietly in his arms, revelling in the feeling of being loved by the one man in the world she had given her heart to.

'They must be looking for us,' she said finally.

The terrace that led out of the ballroom was directly beneath their balcony, and, slipping on a robe, Shefali went out onto the balcony. The party seemed to have descended into general merriment. Far beneath them she could see people laughing and talking, a few couples wrapped in each other's arms.

The faint, tinny sound of someone—probably

Rafiq—speaking into a microphone floated up to them. 'The next item for the festivities was to be the bride and groom cutting the cake—but as we can find neither the bride…'

Another voice—probably Freddy's—chimed in, 'Nor the groom!'

The first voice went, 'The cake has been carved up by the lovely mother of the bride, and if you run across immediately there's a small chance that you might be able to grab a bite. Going, going, *gone*…'

Neil came to stand next to her. He was wearing a pair of pyjama bottoms but his magnificent torso was bare in the moonlight. Shefali took a moment to admire him, and then snuggled into his arms.

'Want to go grab a piece of wedding cake?' he asked teasingly.

She shook her head.

'I want us to stay here, alone with each other for the rest of our lives,' she said dreamily, then looked mischievously up at him. 'But as we can't do that, let's make the best of the time that we do have…'

And they did.

* * * * *

Mills & Boon® Hardback
June 2013

ROMANCE

The Sheikh's Prize	Lynne Graham
Forgiven but not Forgotten?	Abby Green
His Final Bargain	Melanie Milburne
A Throne for the Taking	Kate Walker
Diamond in the Desert	Susan Stephens
A Greek Escape	Elizabeth Power
Princess in the Iron Mask	Victoria Parker
An Invitation to Sin	Sarah Morgan
Too Close for Comfort	Heidi Rice
The Right Mr Wrong	Natalie Anderson
The Making of a Princess	Teresa Carpenter
Marriage for Her Baby	Raye Morgan
The Man Behind the Pinstripes	Melissa McClone
Falling for the Rebel Falcon	Lucy Gordon
Secrets & Saris	Shoma Narayanan
The First Crush Is the Deepest	Nina Harrington
One Night She Would Never Forget	Amy Andrews
When the Cameras Stop Rolling...	Connie Cox

MEDICAL

NYC Angels: Making the Surgeon Smile	Lynne Marshall
NYC Angels: An Explosive Reunion	Alison Roberts
The Secret in His Heart	Caroline Anderson
The ER's Newest Dad	Janice Lynn

0513 GEN STD HB

Mills & Boon® Large Print
June 2013

ROMANCE

Sold to the Enemy	Sarah Morgan
Uncovering the Silveri Secret	Melanie Milburne
Bartering Her Innocence	Trish Morey
Dealing Her Final Card	Jennie Lucas
In the Heat of the Spotlight	Kate Hewitt
No More Sweet Surrender	Caitlin Crews
Pride After Her Fall	Lucy Ellis
Her Rocky Mountain Protector	Patricia Thayer
The Billionaire's Baby SOS	Susan Meier
Baby out of the Blue	Rebecca Winters
Ballroom to Bride and Groom	Kate Hardy

HISTORICAL

Never Trust a Rake	Annie Burrows
Dicing with the Dangerous Lord	Margaret McPhee
Haunted by the Earl's Touch	Ann Lethbridge
The Last de Burgh	Deborah Simmons
A Daring Liaison	Gail Ranstrom

MEDICAL

From Christmas to Eternity	Caroline Anderson
Her Little Spanish Secret	Laura Iding
Christmas with Dr Delicious	Sue MacKay
One Night That Changed Everything	Tina Beckett
Christmas Where She Belongs	Meredith Webber
His Bride in Paradise	Joanna Neil

Mills & Boon® Hardback
July 2013

ROMANCE

His Most Exquisite Conquest	Emma Darcy
One Night Heir	Lucy Monroe
His Brand of Passion	Kate Hewitt
The Return of Her Past	Lindsay Armstrong
The Couple who Fooled the World	Maisey Yates
Proof of Their Sin	Dani Collins
In Petrakis's Power	Maggie Cox
A Shadow of Guilt	Abby Green
Once is Never Enough	Mira Lyn Kelly
The Unexpected Wedding Guest	Aimee Carson
A Cowboy To Come Home To	Donna Alward
How to Melt a Frozen Heart	Cara Colter
The Cattleman's Ready-Made Family	Michelle Douglas
Rancher to the Rescue	Jennifer Faye
What the Paparazzi Didn't See	Nicola Marsh
My Boyfriend and Other Enemies	Nikki Logan
The Gift of a Child	Sue MacKay
How to Resist a Heartbreaker	Louisa George

MEDICAL

Dr Dark and Far-Too Delicious	Carol Marinelli
Secrets of a Career Girl	Carol Marinelli
A Date with the Ice Princess	Kate Hardy
The Rebel Who Loved Her	Jennifer Taylor

0613 GEN STD HB

Mills & Boon® Large Print
July 2013

ROMANCE

Playing the Dutiful Wife	Carol Marinelli
The Fallen Greek Bride	Jane Porter
A Scandal, a Secret, a Baby	Sharon Kendrick
The Notorious Gabriel Diaz	Cathy Williams
A Reputation For Revenge	Jennie Lucas
Captive in the Spotlight	Annie West
Taming the Last Acosta	Susan Stephens
Guardian to the Heiress	Margaret Way
Little Cowgirl on His Doorstep	Donna Alward
Mission: Soldier to Daddy	Soraya Lane
Winning Back His Wife	Melissa McClone

HISTORICAL

The Accidental Prince	Michelle Willingham
The Rake to Ruin Her	Julia Justiss
The Outrageous Belle Marchmain	Lucy Ashford
Taken by the Border Rebel	Blythe Gifford
Unmasking Miss Lacey	Isabelle Goddard

MEDICAL

The Surgeon's Doorstep Baby	Marion Lennox
Dare She Dream of Forever?	Lucy Clark
Craving Her Soldier's Touch	Wendy S. Marcus
Secrets of a Shy Socialite	Wendy S. Marcus
Breaking the Playboy's Rules	Emily Forbes
Hot-Shot Doc Comes to Town	Susan Carlisle